D0590581

HORRiD HENRY
Shows Who's Boss

Vote Henry
OR ELSE !

Francesca Simon

HORRiD HENRY
Shows
Who's Boss

Illustrated by Tony Ross

Orion
Children's Books

For Jake, Amy, Rafi and Daisy

This collection first published in Great Britain in 2010
by Orion Children's Books
a division of the Orion Publishing Group Ltd
Orion House
5 Upper St Martin's Lane
London WC2H 9EA
An Hachette UK Company

3 5 7 9 10 8 6 4 2

Text copyright © Francesca Simon 2005, 2006, 2007, 2008, 2009, 2010
Illustrations copyright © Tony Ross 2005, 2006, 2007, 2008, 2009, 2010

The rights of Francesca Simon and Tony Ross to be identified as
the author and illustrator of this work respectively have been asserted.

All rights reserved. No part of this publication may be reproduced,
stored in a retrieval system, or transmitted, in any form or by any means,
electronic, mechanical, photocopying, recording or otherwise, without
the prior permission of Orion Children's Books.

The Orion Publishing Group's policy is to use papers that are natural,
renewable and recyclable products and made from wood grown in
sustainable forests. The logging and manufacturing processes are expected to
conform to the environmental regulations of the country of origin.

A catalogue record for this book is available from the British Library.

ISBN 978 1 4440 0089 4

Printed in Italy by Printer Trento Srl.

www.orionbooks.co.uk

Contents

HORRiD HENRY'S
Christmas Lunch

'**O**h, handkerchiefs, just what I wanted,' said Perfect Peter. 'Thank you *so* much.'

'Not handkerchiefs *again*,' moaned Horrid Henry, throwing the hankies aside and ripping the paper off the next present in his pile.

'Don't tear the wrapping paper!' squeaked Perfect Peter.

Horrid Henry ripped open the present and groaned.

Yuck (a pen, pencil, and ruler). Yuck (a dictionary). Yuck (gloves). OK (£15 – should have been a lot more). Eeew (a pink bow tie from Aunt Ruby). Eeew (mints). Yum (huge tin of chocolates). Good (five more knights for his army). Very good (a subscription to Gross–Out Fan Club) . . .

And (very very good) a Terminator Gladiator trident . . . and . . .

And . . . where was the rest?

'Is that it?' shrieked Henry.

'You haven't opened my present, Henry,' said Peter. 'I hope you like it.'

Horrid Henry tore off the wrapping. It was a Manners With Maggie calendar.

'Ugh, gross,' said Henry. 'No thank you.'

'Henry!' said Mum. 'That's no way to receive a present.'

11

'I don't care,' moaned Horrid Henry. 'Where's my Zapatron Hip-Hop dinosaur? And where's the rest of the Terminator Gladiator fighting kit? I wanted everything, not just the trident.'

'Maybe next year,' said Mum.

'But I want it now!' howled Henry.

'Henry, you know that "I want doesn't get",' said Peter. 'Isn't that right, Mum?'

'It certainly is,' said Mum. 'And I haven't heard you say thank you, Henry.'

Horrid Henry glared at Peter and sprang. He was a hornet stinging a worm to death.

'WAAAAAAH!' wailed Peter.

'Henry! Stop it or–'

Ding! Dong!

'They're here!' shouted Horrid Henry, leaping up and abandoning his prey. 'That means more presents!'

'Wait, Henry,' said Mum.

But too late. Henry raced to the door and flung it open.

There stood Granny and Grandpa, Prissy Polly, Pimply Paul, and Vomiting Vera.

'Gimme my presents!' he shrieked, snatching a bag of brightly wrapped gifts out of Granny's hand and spilling them on the floor. Now, where were the ones with his name on?

'Merry Christmas, everyone,' said Mum brightly. 'Henry, don't be rude.'

'I'm not being rude,' said Henry. 'I just want my presents. Great, money!' said Henry, beaming. 'Thanks, Granny! But couldn't you add a few pounds and—'

'Henry, don't be horrid!' snapped Dad.

'Let the guests take off their coats,' said Mum.

'Bleeeeech,' said Vomiting Vera, throwing up on Paul.

'Eeeeek,' said Polly.

All the grown-ups gathered in the sitting room to open their gifts.

'Peter, thank you so much for the perfume, it's my favourite,' said Granny.

'I know,' said Peter.

'And what a lovely comic, Henry,' said Granny. 'Mutant Max is my . . . um . . . favourite.'

'Thank you, Henry,' said Grandpa. 'This comic looks very . . . interesting.'

'I'll have it back when you've finished with it,' said Henry.

'Henry!' said Mum, glaring.

For some reason Polly didn't look delighted with her present.

'Eeeek!' squeaked Polly. 'This soap has . . . hairs in it.' She pulled out a long black one.

'That came free,' said Horrid Henry.

'We're getting you toothpaste next year, you little brat,' muttered Pimply Paul under his breath.

Honestly, there was no pleasing some people, thought Horrid Henry indignantly. He'd given Paul a great bar of soap, and he didn't seem thrilled. So much for it's the thought that counts.

'A poem,' said Mum. 'Henry, how lovely.'

'Read it out loud,' said Grandpa.

15

> 'Dear old wrinkly Mum
> Don't be glum
> 'Cause you've got a fat tum
> And an even bigger...'

'Maybe later,' said Mum.
'Another poem,' said Dad. 'Great!'
'Let's hear it,' said Granny.

> 'Dear old baldy Dad—

. . . and so forth,' said Dad, folding Henry's poem quickly.

'Oh,' said Polly, staring at the crystal frog vase Mum and Dad had given her. 'How funny. This

16

looks just like the vase *I* gave Aunt Ruby for Christmas last year.'

'What a coincidence,' said Mum, blushing bright red.

'Great minds think alike,' said Dad quickly.

Dad gave Mum an iron.

'Oh, an iron, just what I always wanted,' said Mum.

Mum gave Dad oven gloves.

'Oh, oven gloves, just what I always wanted,' said Dad.

Pimply Paul gave Prissy Polly a huge power drill.

'Eeeek,' squealed Polly. 'What's this?'

'Oh, that's the Megawatt Superduper Drill-o-matic 670 XM3,' said Paul, 'and just wait till you see the attachments. You're getting those for your birthday.'

'Oh,' said Polly.

Granny gave Grandpa a lovely mug to put his false teeth in.

Grandpa gave Granny a shower cap and a bumper pack of dusters.

'What super presents!' said Mum.

'Yes,' said Perfect Peter. 'I loved every single one of my presents, especially the satsumas and walnuts in my stocking.'

'I didn't,' said Horrid Henry.

'Henry, don't be horrid,' said Dad. 'Who'd like a mince pie?'

'Are they homemade or from the shop?' asked Henry.

'Homemade of course,' said Dad.

'Gross,' said Henry.

'Ooh,' said Polly. 'No, Vera!' she squealed as Vera vomited all over the plate.

'Never mind,' said Mum tightly. 'There's more in the kitchen.'

Horrid Henry was bored. Horrid Henry was fed up. The presents had all been opened. His parents had made him go on a long, boring walk. Dad had confiscated his Terminator trident when he had speared Peter with it.

So, what now?

Grandpa was sitting in the armchair with his pipe, snoring, his tinsel crown slipping over his face.

Prissy Polly and Pimply Paul were squabbling over whose turn it was to change Vera's stinky nappy.

'Eeeek,' said Polly. 'I did it last.'

'I did,' said Paul.

'WAAAAAAAA!' wailed Vomiting Vera.

Perfect Peter was watching Sammy the Snail slithering about on TV.

Horrid Henry snatched the clicker and switched channels.

'Hey, I was watching that!' protested Peter.

'Tough,' said Henry.

Let's see, what was on? 'Tra la la la . . .' Ick! Daffy and her Dancing Daisies.

'Wait! I want to watch!' wailed Peter.

Click. ' . . . and the tension builds as the judges compare tomatoes grown . . . ' Click! ' . . . wish you a Merry Christmas, we wish you . . .' Click! 'Chartres Cathedral is one of the wonders of . . . ' Click!

'HA HA HA HA HA HA HA HA.'

Opera! Click! Why was there nothing good on TV? Just a baby movie about singing cars he'd seen a million times already.

'I'm bored,' moaned Henry. 'And I'm starving.'

He wandered into the kitchen, which looked like a hurricane had swept through.

'When's lunch? I thought we were eating at two. I'm starving.'

'Soon,' said Mum. She looked a little frazzled. 'There's been a little problem with the oven.'

'So when's lunch?' bellowed Horrid Henry.

'When it's ready!' bellowed Dad.

Henry waited. And waited. And waited.

'When's lunch?' asked Polly.

'When's lunch?' asked Paul.

'When's lunch?' asked Peter.

'As soon as the turkey is cooked,' said Dad. He peeked into the oven. He poked the turkey. Then he went pale.

'It's hardly cooked,' he whispered.

'Check the temperature,' said Granny.

Dad checked.

'Oops,' said Dad.

'Never mind, we can start with the sprouts,' said Mum cheerfully.

'That's not the right way to do sprouts,' said Granny. 'You're peeling too many of the leaves off.'

'Yes, Mother,' said Dad.

'That's not the right way to make bread sauce,' said Granny.

'Yes, Mother,' said Dad.

'That's not the right way to make stuffing,' said Granny.

'Yes, Mother,' said Dad.

'That's not the right way to roast potatoes,' said Granny.

'Mother!' yelped Dad. 'Leave me alone!'

'Don't be horrid,' said Granny.

'I'm not being horrid,' said Dad.

'Come along Granny, let's get you a nice drink and leave the chef on his own,' said Mum, steering Granny firmly towards the sitting room. Then she stopped.

'Is something burning?' asked Mum, sniffing.

Dad checked the oven.

'Not in here.'

There was a shriek from the sitting room.

'It's Grandpa!' shouted Perfect Peter.

Everyone ran in.

There was Grandpa, asleep in his chair. A thin column of black smoke rose from the arms. His paper crown, drooping over his pipe, was smoking.

23

'Whh..whh?' mumbled Grandpa, as Mum whacked him with her broom. 'AAARRGH!' he gurgled as Dad threw water over him.

'When's lunch?' screamed Horrid Henry.

'When it's ready,' screamed Dad.

It was dark when Henry's family finally sat down to Christmas lunch. Henry's tummy was rumbling so loudly with hunger he thought the walls would cave in. Henry and Peter made a dash to grab the seat against the wall, furthest from the kitchen.

'Get off!' shouted Henry.

'It's my turn to sit here,' wailed Peter.

'Mine!'

'Mine!'

Slap!

Slap!

'WAAAAAAAAAAA!' screeched Henry.

'WAAAAAAAAAAAA!' wailed Peter.

'Quiet!' screamed Dad.

Mum brought in fresh holly and ivy to decorate the table.

'Lovely,' said Mum, placing the boughs all along the centre.

'Very festive,' said Granny.

'I'm starving!' wailed Horrid Henry. 'This isn't Christmas lunch, it's Christmas dinner.'

'Shhh,' said Grandpa.

The turkey was finally cooked. There were platefuls of stuffing, sprouts, cranberries, bread sauce and peas.

'Smells good,' said Granny.

'Hmmn, boy,' said Grandpa. 'What a feast.'

Horrid Henry was so hungry he could eat the tablecloth.

'Come on, let's eat!' he said.

'Hold on, I'll just get the roast potatoes,' said Dad. Wearing his new oven gloves, he carried in the steaming hot potatoes in a glass roasting dish, and set it in the middle of the table.

'Voila!' said Dad. 'Now, who wants dark meat and who . . .'

'What's that crawling . . . aaaarrrghh!' screamed Polly. 'There are spiders everywhere!'

Millions of tiny spiders were pouring from the holly and crawling all over the table and the food.

'Don't panic!' shouted Pimply Paul, leaping from his chair, 'I know what to do, we just–'

But before he could do anything the glass dish with the roast potatoes exploded.

CRASH!

SMASH!

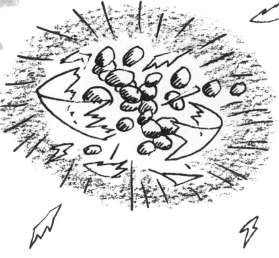

'EEEEEKK!'
screamed Polly.

Everyone stared
at the slivers of glass
glistening all over
the table and the food.

Dad sank down in his chair and covered his eyes.

'Where are we going to get more food?'
whispered Mum.

'I don't know,' muttered Dad.

'I know,' said Horrid Henry, 'let's start with
Christmas pudding and defrost some pizzas.'

Dad opened his eyes.

Mum opened her eyes.

'That,' said Dad, 'is a brilliant idea.'

'I really fancy some pizza,' said Grandpa.

'Me too,' said Granny.

Henry beamed. It wasn't
often his ideas were recognised
for their brilliance.

'Merry Christmas everyone,'
said Horrid Henry. 'Merry
Christmas.'

HORRiD HENRY'S Best Guest List

Mutant Max

Marvin the Maniac

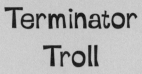

Terminator Troll

Killer Boy Rats

HORRID HENRY'S
Arch Enemy

'**B**e bop a lu la!'
boomed Jazzy Jim,
bebopping round
the class and bouncing to the
beat.

'One day, my prince will
come . . .' warbled Singing
Soraya.

'Bam bam bam bam bam!'
drummed Horrid Henry,
crashing his books up and
down on his table top.

'Class! Settle down!' shouted Miss Battle-Axe.

'Be bop a lu la!' boomed Jazzy Jim.

'One day, my prince will come . . .' warbled Singing
Soraya.

'Bam bam bam bam bam!'
drummed Horrid Henry.

'Jim!' barked Miss Battle-
Axe. 'Stop yowling. Soraya! Stop
singing. Henry! Stop banging or
everyone will miss playtime.'

'Be bop—' faltered Jim.

'. . . prince will—' squeaked
Soraya.

'Bam bam bam bam bam,'
drummed Horrid Henry. He
was Mad Moon Madison, crazy
drummer for the Mouldy Drumsticks, whipping the
shrieking crowd into a frenzy–

'HENRY!' bellowed Miss Battle-Axe. 'STOP THAT NOISE!'

What did that ungrateful fan mean, noise? What noise? This wasn't noise, this was great music, this was— Mad Moon Madison looked up from his drum kit. Whoops.

Silence.

Miss Battle-Axe glared at her class. Oh, for the good old days, when teachers could whack horrible children with rulers.

'Linda! Stop snoring. Graham! Stop drooling. Bert! Where's your chair?'

'I dunno,' said Beefy Bert.

There was a new boy standing next to Miss Battle-Axe. His brown hair was tightly slicked back. His shoes were polished. He carried a trumpet and a calculator. Yuck! He looked like a complete idiot. Horrid Henry looked away. And then looked back. Funny, there was something familiar about that boy. The way he stood with his nose in the air. The horrid little smirk on his face. He looked like – he looked just like – oh no,

please no, it couldn't
be – Bossy Bill! Bossy
Bill!!

'Class, we have a
new boy,' said Miss
Battle-Axe, doing her
best to twist her thin
lips into a welcoming
smile. 'I need someone
to look after him and
show him around. Who
would like to be Bill's
friend for the day?'

Everyone put up
their hand. Everyone
but Horrid Henry. Uggh. Bossy Bill. What kind of
cruel joke was this?

Bossy Bill was the horrible, stuck-up son of Dad's boss. Horrid Henry hated Bill. Uggh! Yuck! Just thinking about Bill made Henry gag.

Henry had a suspicion he wasn't Bill's favourite person, either. The last time they'd met, Henry had tricked Bill into photocopying his bottom.

Bill had got into trouble. Big, big trouble.

Miss Battle-Axe scanned the sea of waving hands.

'Me!' shouted Moody Margaret.

'Me!' shouted Kind Kasim.

'Me!' shouted Weepy William.

'There's an empty seat next to Henry,' said Miss Battle-Axe, pointing. 'Henry will look after you.'

NO, thought Henry.

'Waaaaaa,' wailed Weepy William. 'I didn't get picked.'

'Go and sit down, Bill,' continued Miss Battle-Axe. 'Class, silent reading from page 12.'

Bossy Bill walked between the tables towards Horrid Henry.

Maybe he won't recognise me, thought Henry hopefully. After all, it was a long time ago.

Suddenly Bill stopped. His face contorted with loathing.

Oops.

He recognised me, thought Horrid Henry.

Bill marched, scowling, to the seat next to Henry and sat down. His nose wrinkled as if he smelled a stinky smell.

'You say one word about what happened at my dad's office and I'll tell my dad,' hissed Bill.

'You say one word to your dad and I'll tell everyone at school you photocopied your bottom,' hissed Henry.

'Then I'll tell on you!'

'I'll tell on you!'

Bill shoved Henry.

Henry shoved Bill.

'He shoved me, miss!' shouted Bossy Bill.

'He shoved me first!' shouted Horrid Henry.

'Henry!' said Miss Battle-Axe. 'I am shocked and appalled. Is this how you welcome a new boy to our class?'

It is when the boy is Bossy Bill, thought Henry grimly.

He glared at Bill.

Bill glared at Henry.

'My old school's a lot better than this dump,' hissed Bossy Bill.

'So why don't you go back there?' hissed Henry. 'No one's stopping you.'

'Maybe I will,' said Bill.

Horrid Henry's heart leapt. Was there a chance he could get Bill to leave?

'You don't want to stay here – we get four hours of homework a night,' lied Henry.

'So?' said Bill. 'My old school gave you five hours.'

'The food's horrible.'

'Big deal,' said Bill.

'And Miss Battle-Axe is the meanest teacher in the world.'

'What did you say, Henry?' demanded Miss Battle-Axe's ice cold dagger voice.

'I just told Bill you were the keenest teacher in the

world,' said Henry quickly.

'No he didn't,' said Bill. 'He said you were the meanest.'

'Keenest,' said Henry.

'Meanest,' said Bill.

Miss Battle-Axe glared at Horrid Henry.

'I'm watching you, Henry. Now get back to work.'

DING! DING! DING!

Hurray! Saved by the playtime bell.

Horrid Henry jumped from his seat. Maybe he could escape Bill if he ran out of class fast enough.

Henry pushed and shoved his way into the hall.

Free! Free at last!

'Hey!' came an unwelcome voice beside him. A sweaty hand pulled on his shirt.

'The teacher said you're supposed to show me around,' said Bossy Bill.

'OK, here are the toilets,' snarled Horrid Henry, waving his hand in the direction of the girls' loos. 'And the photocopier's in the office,' he added, pointing. 'Why don't you try it out?'

Bill scowled.

'I'm going to tell my dad that you attacked me,' said Bill. 'In fact, I'm going to tell my dad every single bad thing you do in school. Then he'll tell yours and you'll get into trouble. And won't I laugh.'

Henry's blood boiled. What had he ever done to

deserve Bossy Bill butting into his life? A spy in his class. Could school get any worse?

Aerobic Al jogged past.

'Henry photocopied his bottom at my dad's office,' said Bill loudly. 'Boy, did he get into trouble.'

AAARRRGGHHH!

'That's a lie,' said Horrid Henry hotly. 'Bill did, not me.'

'Yeah right, Henry,' said Dizzy Dave.

'Big bottom!' shrieked Moody Margaret.

'Big big bottom!' shrieked Sour Susan.

Bill smirked.

'Bye, big bottom,' said Bill. 'Don't forget, I'm watching you,' he hissed.

Henry sat down by himself on the broken bench in the secret garden. He had to get Bill out of his class. School was horrible enough without someone evil like Bill spying on him and spreading foul rumours. His life would be ruined. He had to get rid of Bill-fast. But how?

Maybe he could get Bill to run screaming from school and never come back. Wow, thought Horrid Henry. Wouldn't that be wonderful? Bye bye Bossy Bill.

Or maybe he could get Bill to photocopy his bottom again. Probably not, thought Horrid Henry regretfully. Aha! He could trick Bill into dancing nude on Miss Battle-Axe's desk singing 'I'm a busy bumblebee – buzz buzz buzz.' That would be sure to get him expelled.

The only trouble was – how?

I've got to think of something, thought Horrid Henry desperately. I've just got to.

'Henry,' said Dad the next evening, 'my boss tells me you've been picking on his son. Bill was very upset.'

'He's picking on me,' protested Henry.

'And that you were told off in class for shouting out.'

'No way,' lied Henry.

'And that you broke Andrew's pencil.'

'That was an accident,' said Henry.

'And that you called Margaret nitty-face.'

'I didn't,' wailed Henry. 'Bill's lying.'

'I want you to be on your best behaviour from now on,' said Dad. 'How do you think I feel hearing these reports about you from my boss? I've never been so embarrassed in my life.'

'Who cares?' screamed Horrid Henry. 'What about me?'

'Go to your room!' shouted Dad.

'FINE!' yelled Horrid Henry, slamming the door behind him as hard as he could. I'll beat you, Bill, thought Henry, if it's the last thing I do.

Horrid Henry tried teasing Bill. Horrid Henry tried pinching Bill. He tried spreading rumours about Bill. He even tried getting Bill to punch him so Bill would be suspended.

But nothing worked. Henry just got into more and more trouble.

On Monday Dad told Henry off for making rude noises in class.

On Tuesday Dad told Henry off for talking during storytime.

On Wednesday Dad told Henry off for not handing in his homework.

On Thursday Mum and Dad yelled at Henry for chewing gum in class, passing notes to Ralph, throwing food, jiggling his desk, pulling Margaret's hair, running down the hall and kicking a football into the back playground. Then they banned him from the computer for a week. And all because of Bossy Bill.

Horrid Henry slunk into class. It was hopeless. Bill was here to stay. Horrid Henry would just have to grit his teeth and bear it.

Miss Battle-Axe started explaining electricity. Henry looked around the classroom.

Speaking of Bill, where was he?

Maybe he has rabies, thought Horrid Henry hopefully. Or fallen down the toilet. Better still, maybe he'd been kidnapped by aliens.

Or maybe he'd been expelled. Yes! H enry could see it now. Bill on his knees in Mrs Oddbod's office, begging to stay. Mrs Oddbod pointing to the door:

'Out of this school, you horrible monster! How dare you spy on Henry, our best pupil?'

'NOOO!' Bill would wail.

'BEGONE, WRETCH!' commanded Mrs Oddbod. And out went Bossy Bill, snivelling, where armed guards were waiting to truss him up and take him to prison. That must be what had happened.

Henry smiled.

Oh joyful day! No more Bossy Bill, thought Horrid Henry happily, stretching his legs under his Bill-free table and taking a deep breath of Bill-free air.

'Henry!' snapped Miss Battle-Axe. 'Come here.'

What now?

Slowly Horrid Henry heaved himself out of his chair and scuffed his way to Miss Battle-Axe's desk, where she was busy slashing at homework with a bright red pen.

'Bill has a sore throat,' said Miss Battle-Axe.

Rats, thought Horrid Henry. Where was the black

plague when you needed it?

'His parents want him to have his homework assignments so he doesn't fall behind while he's ill,' said Miss Battle-Axe. 'If only *all* parents were so conscientious. Please give this maths worksheet to your father to give to Bill's dad.'

She handed Henry a piece of paper with ten multiplication sums on it and a large envelope.

'OK,' said Henry dully. Not even the thought of Bill lying in bed doing sums could cheer him up. All too soon Bill would be back. He was stuck with Bill for ever.

That night Horrid Henry glanced at Bill's maths worksheet. Ten sums. Not enough, really, he thought. Why should Bill be bored in bed with nothing to do but watch TV, and read comics, and eat crisps?

And then Horrid Henry smiled. Bill wanted homework? Perhaps Henry could help. Tee hee, thought Horrid Henry, sitting down at the computer.

TAP
TAP
TAP

HOMEWERK
Rite a storee abowt yor day. 20 pages long.

Ha ha ha, that will keep Bill busy, thought Horrid Henry. Now, what else? What else?
Aha!

Give ten reesons why watching TV is better than reading

NEW MATHS
When does 2 + 2 = 5 ?
When 2 is big enough.
Now explain why:
2+3=6
7-3=5

It was a lot
more fun making
up homework than
doing it, thought
Horrid Henry
happily.

SPELLING:
Lern how to spel these words fer a test on Tuesday.
Terrantula
Stinkbomb
Moosli
Doovay
Screem
Intergalactik

SCEINSE
Gravity: does it work?

Drop an egg from a hight of 30 mm onto your mum or dad's hed.

Record if it breaks. Drop another egg from a hight of 60 mm onto yor carpet. Does this egg break? Try this xperiment at least 12 times all over yor house.

Now that's what I call homework, thought Horrid Henry. He printed out the worksheets, popped them in the envelope with Miss Battle-Axe's sheet of sums, sealed it, and gave it to Dad.

'Bill's homework,' said Henry. 'Miss Battle-Axe asked me to give it to you to give to Bill's dad.'

'I'll make sure he gets it,' said Dad, putting the envelope in his briefcase. 'I'm glad to see you're becoming friends with Bill.'

Dad looked stern.

'I've got some bad news for you, Henry,' said Dad the next day.

Horrid Henry froze. What was he going to get told off about now? Oh no. Had Dad found out about what he'd done at lunchtime?

'I'm afraid Bill won't be coming back to your

school,' said Dad. 'His parents have removed him. Something about new maths and a gravity experiment that went wrong.'

Horrid Henry's mouth opened. No sound came out.

'Wha–?' gasped Horrid Henry.

'Gravity experiment?' said Mum. 'What gravity experiment?'

'Different science group,' said Henry quickly.

'Oh,' said Mum.

'Oh,' said Dad.

A lovely warm feeling spread from Henry's head all the way down to his toes.

'So Bill's not coming back?'

'No,' said Dad. 'I'm sorry that you've lost a friend.'

'I'll live,' beamed Horrid Henry.

Extra Science Experiments

Is water wet?

Pour water all over your younger brother. Check him. Is he wet? If yes, you have proved scientifically that water is wet. If he is dry, try again using twice as much water.

Is it true that too much sugar rots your teeth?

Eat lots of sweets every day for a month. Check your teeth at night. Have they rotted? If not, you have proven scientifically that sugar is good for you!

Seeds: do they grow?

Cover your younger
brother's or sister's
arms and legs in dirt
and plant seeds.
Water every day.
Describe what grows.

MOODY MARGARET'S
Makeover

'**W**atch out, Gurinder! You're smearing your nail varnish,' screeched Moody Margaret. 'Violet! Don't touch your face – you're spoiling all my hard work. Susan! Sit still.'

'I am sitting still,' said Sour Susan. 'Stop pulling my hair.'

'I'm not pulling your hair,' hissed Margaret. 'I'm styling it.'

'Ouch!' squealed Susan. 'You're hurting me.'

'I am not, crybaby.'

'I'm not a crybaby,' howled Susan.

Moody Margaret sighed loudly.

'Not everyone can be naturally beautiful like me. Some people'– she glared at Susan – 'have to work at it.'

'You're not beautiful,' said Sour Susan, snorting.

'I am too,' said Margaret, preening herself.

'Are not,' said Susan. 'On the ugly scale of 1 to 10, with 1 being the ugliest,

wartiest, toad, you're a 2.'

'Huh!' said Margaret. 'Well, *you're* so ugly you're minus 1. They don't have an ugly enough scale for *you*.'

'I want my money back!' shrieked Susan.

'No way!' shrieked Margaret. 'Now sit down and shut up.'

Across the wall in the next garden, deep inside the branches hiding the top secret entrance of the Purple Hand fort, a master spy pricked up his ears.

Money? Had he heard the word *money?*

What was going on next door?

Horrid Henry zipped out of his fort and dashed to the low wall separating his garden from Margaret's. Then he stared. And stared some more. He'd seen many weird things in his life. But nothing as weird as this.

Moody Margaret, Sour Susan, Lazy Linda, Vain Violet and Gorgeous Gurinder were sitting in Margaret's garden. Susan had rollers tangling her pink hair. Violet had blue mascara all over her face. Linda was covered in gold glitter. There was spilt nail varnish, face powder, and broken lipstick all over Margaret's patio.

Horrid Henry burst out laughing.

'Are you playing clowns?' said Henry.

'Huh, that's how much *you* know, Henry,' said Margaret. '*I'm* doing makeovers.'

'What's that?' said Henry.

'It's when you change how people look, dummy,' said Margaret.

'I knew that,' lied Henry. 'I just wanted to see if you did.'

Margaret waved a leaflet in his face.

Margaret's
Magnificent Makeovers

I can make you beautiful!
Yes, even YOU.
No one too old or too ugly.
Only £1 for a new you!!!!!

Hurry!

Special offer ends soon!!!!!!!!!!

Makeovers? *Makeovers?* What an incredibly stupid idea. Who'd pay to have a moody old grouch like Margaret smear gunk all over their face? Ha! No one.

Horrid Henry started laughing and pointing.

Vain Violet looked like a demon with red and blue and purple gloop all over her face. Gorgeous Gurinder looked as if a paint pot had been poured down her cheeks. Linda's hair looked as if she'd been struck by lightning.

But Violet wasn't screaming and yanking Margaret's hair out. Instead she handed Margaret – *money*.

'Thanks, Margaret, I look amazing,' said Vain Violet, admiring herself in the mirror. Henry waited for the mirror to crack.

It didn't.

'Thanks, Margaret,' said Gurinder. 'I look so fantastic I hardly recognise myself.' And she also handed Margaret a pound.

Two whole pounds? Were they mad?

'Are you getting ready for the Monster's Ball?' jeered Henry.

'Shut up, Henry,' said Vain Violet.

'Shut up, Henry,' said Gorgeous Gurinder.

'You're just jealous because I'm going to be rich and you're not,' said Margaret. 'Nah nah ne nah nah.'

'Why don't we give Henry a makeover?' said Violet.

'Good idea,' said Moody Margaret. 'He could sure use one.'

'Yeah,' said Sour Susan.

Horrid Henry took a step back.

Margaret advanced towards him wielding nail varnish and a hairbrush. Violet followed clutching a lipstick, spray dye and other instruments of torture.

Yikes! Horrid Henry nipped back to the safety of his fort as fast as he could, trying to ignore the horrible, cackling laughter.

He sat on his Purple Hand throne and scoffed some extra tasty chocolate biscuits from the secret stash he'd nicked from Margaret yesterday. Makeovers! Ha! How dumb could you get? Trust a pea-brained grouch like Margaret to come up with such a stupid idea. Who in their right mind would want a makeover?

On the other hand . . .

Horrid Henry had actually seen Margaret being paid. And good money, too, just for smearing some coloured gunk onto people's faces and yanking their hair about.

Hmmmn.

Horrid Henry started to think. Maybe Margaret did have a little eensy-weensy teeny-tiny bit of a good idea. And, naturally, anything she could do, Henry could do much, much better.

Margaret obviously didn't know the first thing about makeovers, so why should *she* make all that money, thought Horrid Henry indignantly. He'd steal – no, *borrow* – her idea and do it better. Much much better. He'd make people look *really* fantastic.

Henry's Makeovers. Henry's Marvellous Makeovers. Henry's Miraculous Makeovers.

He'd be rich! With some false teeth and red marker he could turn Miss Battle-Axe into a vampire. Mrs Oddbod could be a perfect Dracula. And wouldn't Stuck-Up Steve be improved after a short visit from the Makeover Magician? Even Aunt Ruby wouldn't recognise him when Henry had finished. Tee hee.

First, he needed supplies. That was easy: Mum had
tons of gunk for smearing all over her face. And if he
ran out he could always use crayons and glue.

Horrid Henry dashed to the bathroom and helped
himself to a few handfuls of Mum's makeup. What on
earth did she need all this stuff for, thought Henry,
piling it into a bag. About time someone cleared out
this drawer. Then
he wrote a few
leaflets.

Horrid
Henry, Makeover
Magician, was
ready for business.

All he needed

were some customers. Preferably rich, ugly customers.
Now, where could he find some of those?

Henry strolled into the sitting room. Dad was reading on the sofa. Mum was working at the computer.

Horrid Henry looked at his aged, wrinkly, boring old parents. Bleeeeccch!

Boy, could they be improved, thought Henry. How could he tactfully persuade these potential customers that they needed his help – fast?

'Mum,' said Henry, 'you know Great-Aunt Greta?'

'Yes,' said Mum.

'Well, you're starting to look just like her.'

'What?' said Mum.

'Yup,' said Horrid Henry, 'old and ugly. Except–' he peered at her, 'you have more wrinkles.'

'*What?*' squeaked Mum.

'And Dad looks like a gargoyle,' said Henry.

'Huh?' said Dad.

'Only scarier,' said Henry. 'But don't worry, I can help.'

'Oh really?' said Mum.

'Oh really?' said Dad.

'Yeah,' said Henry, 'I'm doing makeovers.'

He handed Mum and Dad a leaflet.

Are you ugly?

Are you very very ugly?
Do you look like the creature from the black lagoon? (Only worse?)

Then today is your lucky day!

HENRY'S
MARVELLOUS MAKEOVERS.

Only £2 for an exciting new you!!!!!!

'So, how many makeovers would you like?' said Horrid Henry. 'Ten? Twenty? Maybe more 'cause you're so old and need a lot of work to fix you.'

'Make over someone else,' said Mum, scowling.

'Make over someone else,' said Dad, scowling.

Boy, talk about ungrateful, thought Horrid Henry.

'Me first!'

'No me!'

Screams were coming from Margaret's garden. Kung-Fu Kate and Singing Soraya were about to become her latest victims. Well, not if Henry could help it.

'Step right up, get your makeovers here!' shouted Henry. 'Miracle Makeovers, from an expert. Only £2 for a brand new you.'

'Leave my customers alone, copycat!' hissed Moody Margaret, holding out her hand to snatch Kate's pound.

Henry ignored her.

'You look boring, Kate,' said Henry. 'Why don't you let a *real* expert give you a makeover?'

'You?' said Kate.

'Two pounds and you'll look completely different,' said Horrid Henry. 'Guaranteed.'

'Margaret's only charging £1,' said Kate.

'My special offer today is 75p for the first makeover,' said Henry quickly. 'And free beauty advice,' he added.

Soraya looked up. Kate stood up from Margaret's chair.

'Such as?' scowled Margaret. 'Go on, tell us.'

Eeeek. What on earth was a beauty tip? If your face is dirty, wash it? Use a nit comb? Horrid Henry had no idea.

'Well, in your case wear a bag over your head,' said Horrid Henry. 'Or a bucket.'

Susan snickered.

'Ha ha, very funny,' snapped Margaret. 'Come on, Kate. Don't let him trick you. I'm the makeover expert.'

'I'm going to try Henry,' said Kate.

'Me too,' said Soraya.

Yippee! His first customers. Henry stuck out his tongue at Margaret.

Kung-Fu Kate and Singing Soraya climbed over the wall and sat down on the bench at the picnic table. Henry opened his makeover bag and got to work.

'No peeking,' said Henry. 'I want you to be surprised.'

Henry smeared and coated, primped and coloured, slopped and glopped. This was easy!

'I'm so beautiful – hoo hoo hoo,' hummed Soraya.

'Aren't you going to do my hair?' said Kung-Fu Kate.

'Naturally,' said Horrid Henry.

He emptied a pot of glue on her head and

scrunched it around.

'What have you put in?' said Kate.

'Secret hair potion,' said Henry.

'What about *me*?' said Soraya.

'No problem,' said Henry, shovelling in some red paint.

A bit of black here, a
few blobs of red there, a
smear of purple and . . .
way hey!

Henry stood back to
admire his handiwork.
Wow! Kung-Fu Kate
looked *completely* different.
So did Singing Soraya. Next time he'd charge £10.
The moment people saw them everyone would want

one of Henry's
marvellous
makeovers.

'You look
amazing,' said
Horrid Henry.
He had no idea

he was such a brilliant makeover artist. Customers
would be queueing for his services. He'd need a bigger
piggybank.

'There, just like the Mummy, Frankenstein, *and* a
vampire,' said Henry, handing Kate a mirror.

'AAAARRrrggggGHHH!'

screamed Kung-Fu Kate.

Soraya snatched the mirror.

'AAAARRRɢɢɢɢGHHH!'

screamed Singing Soraya.

Horrid Henry stared at them. Honestly, there was no pleasing some people.

'NOOoooooooo!'

squealed Kung-Fu Kate.

'But I thought you wanted to look amazing,' said Henry.

'Amazingly good! Not scary!' wailed Kate.

'Has anyone seen my new lipsticks?' said Mum. 'I could have sworn I put them in the—'

She caught sight of Soraya and Kate.

'AAAAAAARRRʀɢɢɢɢGHHHH!'

screeched Mum. 'Henry! How could you be so horrid? Go to your room.'

'But . . . but . . . ' gasped Horrid Henry. It was so unfair. Was it his fault his stupid customers didn't know when they looked great?

Henry stomped up the stairs. Then he sighed. Maybe he did need a

little more makeover practice before he opened for
business.

Now, where could he find someone to practise on?

'I got an A on my spelling test,' said Perfect Peter.

'I got a gold star for having the tidiest drawer,' said
Tidy Ted.

'And I got in the Good as Gold book again,' said
Goody-Goody Gordon.

Henry burst
into Peter's
bedroom.

'I'm doing
makeovers,' said
Horrid Henry.
'Who wants to go
first?'

'Uhhmmm,'
said Peter.

'Uhhmmm,'s aid Ted.

'We're going to Sam's birthday party today,' said
Gordon.

'Even better,' said Henry beaming. 'I can make you
look great for the party. Who's first?'

HORRID HENRY'S
Marvellous Makeovers

BEFORE

AFTER

BEFORE

AFTER

No one too ugly to be improved!

BEFORE

AFTER

BEFORE

AFTER

HORRID HENRY'S
Newspaper

'It's not fair!' howled Horrid Henry.

'I want a Hip-Hop Robot dog!'

Horrid Henry needed money. Lots and lots and lots of money. His parents didn't need money, and yet they had loads more than he did. It was so unfair. Why was he so brilliant at *spending* money, and so bad at *getting* money?

And now Mum and Dad refused to buy him something he desperately needed.

'You have plenty of toys,' said Mum.

'Which you never play with,' said Dad.

'That's 'cause they're all so boring!' screeched Henry. 'I want a robot dog!'

'Too expensive,' said Mum.

'Too noisy,' said Dad.

'But *everyone* has a Hip-Hop Robot Dog,' whined Henry. 'Everyone but *me*.'

Horrid Henry stomped out of the room. How could he get some money?

Wait. Maybe he could *persuade* Peter to give him some. Peter always had tons of cash because he never bought anything.

Yes! He could hold Peter's Bunnykins for ransom.

He could tell Peter his room was haunted and get Peter to pay him for ghostbusting. He could make Peter donate to Henry's favourite charity, Child in Need . . . Hip-Hop Robot Dog, here I come, thought Horrid Henry, bursting into Peter's bedroom.

Perfect Peter and Tidy Ted were whispering together on the floor. Papers were scattered all around them.

'You can't come in my room,' said Peter.

'Yes I can,' said Henry, ''cause I'm already in. Pooh, your room stinks.'

'That's 'cause you're in it,' said Peter.

Henry decided to ignore this insult.

'Whatcha doing?'

'Nothing,' said Peter.

'We're writing our own newspaper like Mrs Oddbod suggested in assembly,' said Ted. 'We've even got a *Tidy with Ted* column,' he added proudly.

'A snooze paper, you mean,' said Henry.

'It is not,' said Peter.

Henry snorted. 'What's it called?'

'*The Best Boys' Busy Bee*,' said Peter.

'What a stupid name,' said Henry.

'It's not a stupid name,' said Peter. 'Miss Lovely said it was perfect.'

'Peter, I have a great idea for your paper,' said Henry.

'What?' said Peter cautiously.

'You can use your newspaper for Fluffy's cat litter tray.'

'MUUUM!' wailed Peter. 'Henry's being mean to me.'

'Don't be horrid, Henry!' shouted Mum.

'Peter is a poopsicle, Peter is a poopsicle,' chanted Henry.

But then Peter did something strange. Instead of screaming for Mum, Peter started writing.

'Now everyone who buys my newspaper will know how horrid you are,' said Peter, putting down his pencil.

Buy? *Buy?*

'We're selling it in school tomorrow,' said Ted. 'Miss Lovely said we could.'

Sell? *Sell?*

'Lemme see that,' said Henry, yanking the paper out of Peter's hands.

The *Busy Bee's* headline read:

> ## PETER IN THE
> ## GOOD AS GOLD BOOK FOR THE
> ## FOURTH TIME THIS MONTH

Horrid Henry snorted. What a worm. Then his eye caught the second headline:

'You're going to . . . *sell* this?' spluttered Henry.

> ## COMPUTER BAN FOR
> ## HORRID BOY
>
> Henry was banned from playing games on the computer today because he was mean to his brother Peter and called him wibble pants and poopsicle. The Busy Bee hopes Henry has learned his lesson and will stop being such a big meanie.

His name would be mud. Worse than mud. Everyone would know what a stupid toad brother he had. Worse, some people might even *believe* Peter's lies.

And then suddenly Horrid Henry had a brilliant, spectacular idea. He'd write his *own* newspaper. Everyone would want to buy it. He'd be rich!

He could call his newspaper *The Hourly Howler* and charge 25p a copy. If he could write seven editions a day, and sell each copy to 500 people, he'd make . . . he'd make . . . well, multiplication was never his best subject, but he could make *tons* of money!!!!!!

On the other hand, writing seven newspapers a day, every day, seemed an awful lot of work. An awful, awful lot of work. Perhaps *The Daily Digger* was the way to go. He'd charge a lot more per copy, and do a lot less work. Yes!

Hmmn. Perhaps *The Weekly Warble* would be better. No, *The Monthly Moaner*.

Maybe just *The Purple Hand Basher*.

The Basher! What a great name for a great paper!

Now, what should his newspaper have? News of course. All about Henry's triumphs. And gossip and quizzes and sport.

First, I need a great headline, thought Horrid Henry.

What about: PETER IS A WORM. Tempting, thought Henry, but old news: everyone already knows that Peter is a worm. What could he tell his readers that they *didn't* know?

After all, news didn't have to be true, did it? Just *new*. And boy did he have some brand-new news!

PETER SENT TO PRISON The world's toadiest brother has been found guilty of being a worm and taken straight to prison. He was sentenced to live on bread and water for three years. *The Basher* says: 'It should have been ten years.'

SECRET CLUB COLLAPSES

The Secret Club has collapsed. 'Margaret is
such a moody old bossy-boots no one wants to
be in her club any more,' said Susan.

'Goodbye, grump-face,' said Gurinder.

Right, that was the news section taken care of.
Now, for some good gossip.

But what gossip? What scandal? Sadly, Horrid
Henry didn't know any horrid rumours. But a gossip
columnist needed to write something . . .

MRS ODDBOD IN
BIKINI SHOCK

Mrs Oddbod was seen
strolling down the High
Street wearing a new
yellow polka dot bikini.
Is this any way for a head
teacher to behave?

MISS LOVELY IN
NOSE PICK HORROR

Oh dear, Miss
Lydia Lovely picks
her nose.

'I saw her do
it in class,' says
Prisoner Peter.

'But she said it
was her nose and
she would pick it
if she wanted to.'

GUESS WHO?

Which soggy swimming teacher was seen dancing the cha-cha-cha with which old battle-axe?

NIT NURSE HAS NITS!

Nitty Nora, Bug Explorer was sent home from school with nits last week. Whoopee! No more bug-busting!

TEACHER IN TOILET TERROR

Terrible screams rang out from the boys' toilets yesterday. 'Help! Help! There's a monster in the loo!' screamed the crazed teacher Miss Boudicca Battle-Axe. 'It's got hairy scary claws and three heads!!'

That's enough great gossip for one issue, thought Horrid Henry. Now, what else, what else? A bit about sports and he was done. In tomorrow's edition, he'd add a comic strip: The adventures of Peter the Nappy. And a quiz:

WHO HAS THE SMELLIEST PANTS IN SCHOOL?
A. Peter
B. Margaret
C. Susan
D. All of the above!

Yippee! thought Horrid Henry. I'm going to be rich, rich, rich, rich, rich.

The next morning Henry made sure he got to school bright and early. Hip-hop Robot, here I come, thought Horrid Henry, lugging a huge pile of *Bashers* into the playground. Then he stopped.

A terrible sight met his eyes.

Moody Margaret and Sour Susan were standing in the school playground waving big sheets of paper.

'Step right up, read all about it, Margaret made Captain of the school football team,' bellowed Moody Margaret. 'Get your *Daily Dagger* right here. Only 25p!'

What a copycat, thought Horrid Henry. He was outraged.

'Who'd want to read *that*?' sneered Horrid Henry.

'Everyone,' said Susan.

Horrid Henry snatched a copy.

'That'll be 25p, Henry,' said Margaret.

Henry ignored her. The headline read:

MARGARET TRIUMPHS

Margaret, the best footballer in school history, beat out her puny opposition to become captain of the school football team! Well done Margaret! Everyone cheered for hours when Mrs Oddbod announced the glorious news.

Margaret gave an exclusive interview to the *Daily Dagger*:

'It's hard being as amazing as I am,' said Margaret. 'So many people are jealous, especially pongy pants pimples like Henry.'

'What a load of rubbish,' said Horrid Henry, scrunching up Margaret's newspaper.

'Our customers don't think so,' said Margaret. 'I'm making *loads* of loot. Before you know it *I'll* have the first Hip-Hop Robot Dog. And you-ooooo won't,' she chanted.

'We'll see about that,' said Horrid Henry. 'Teacher in toilet terror! Read all about it!' he hollered. 'All the news and gossip. Only 25p.'

'News! News!' screeched Margaret. 'Step right up, step right up! Only 24p.'

'Buy the *Busy Bee*!' piped Peter. 'Only 5p.'

Rude Ralph bought a *Basher*. So did Dizzy Dave and Jolly Josh.

Lazy Linda approached Margaret.

'Oy, Linda, don't buy that rubbish,' shouted Henry. '*I've* got the best news and gossip.' Henry whispered in Linda's ear. Her jaw dropped and she handed Henry 25p.

'Don't listen to him!' squealed Margaret.

'Buy the *Busy Bee*,' trilled Perfect Peter. 'Free vegetable chart.'

'Margaret, did you see what Henry wrote about you?' gasped Gorgeous Gurinder.

'What?' said Margaret, grabbing a *Basher*.

SPORTS

SHOCK FOOTBALL NEWS

There was shock all round when Henry wasn't made captain of the school football team.

'It's an outrage,' said Dave.

'Disgusting,' said Soraya.

The Basher was lucky enough to get an exclusive interview with Henry.

'Not making me captain just goes to show what an idiot that old carrot-nose Miss Battle-Axe is,' says Henry.

The Basher says: **Make Henry captain!**

'What!' screamed Margaret. 'Dave and Soraya never said *that.*'

'They thought it,' said Henry. He glared at Moody Margaret.

Moody Margaret glared at Horrid Henry.

Henry's hand reached out to pull Margaret's hair.

Margaret's foot reached out to kick Henry's leg.

Suddenly Mrs Oddbod walked into the playground. There was a stern-looking man with her, wearing a suit and carrying a notebook. Miss Battle-Axe and Miss Lovely followed.

Aha, new customers, thought Horrid Henry, as they headed towards him.

'Get your school paper here!' hollered Henry. 'Only 50p.'

'News! News!' screeched Margaret. 'Step right up, step right up! 49p.'

'Buy the *Busy Bee!*' trilled Peter. 'Only 5p.'

'Well, well,' said the strange man. 'What have we here, Mrs Oddbod?'

Mrs Oddbod beamed. 'Just three of our best students showing how enterprising they are,' she said.

Horrid Henry thought his ears had fallen off. *Best* student? And why was Mrs Oddbod smiling at him? Mrs Oddbod *never* smiled at him.

'Peter, why don't you tell the inspector what you're doing,' said Miss Lovely.

'I've written my own newspaper to raise money for the school,' said Perfect Peter.

'Very impressive, Mrs Oddbod,' said the school inspector, smiling. 'Very impressive. And what about you, young man?' he added, turning to Henry.

'I'm selling my newspaper for a Child in Need,'
said Horrid Henry. In need of a Hip-Hop Robot, he
thought. 'How many do you want to buy?'

The school inspector handed over 50p and took a
paper.

'I love school newspapers,' he said, starting to read.
'You find out so much about what's really happening
at a school.'

The school
inspector gasped.
Then he turned to
Mrs Oddbod.

'What do you
know about a yellow
polka dot bikini?' said
the Inspector.

'Yellow . . . polka . . . dot . . . bikini?' said Mrs
Oddbod.

'Cha-cha-cha?' choked Miss Battle-Axe.

'Nose-picking?' gasped Miss Lovely.

'But what's the point of writing news that everyone
knows?' protested Horrid Henry afterwards in Mrs
Oddbod's office. 'News should be *new*.'

Just wait till tomorrow's edition . . .

The Adventures of
PETER THE NAPPY

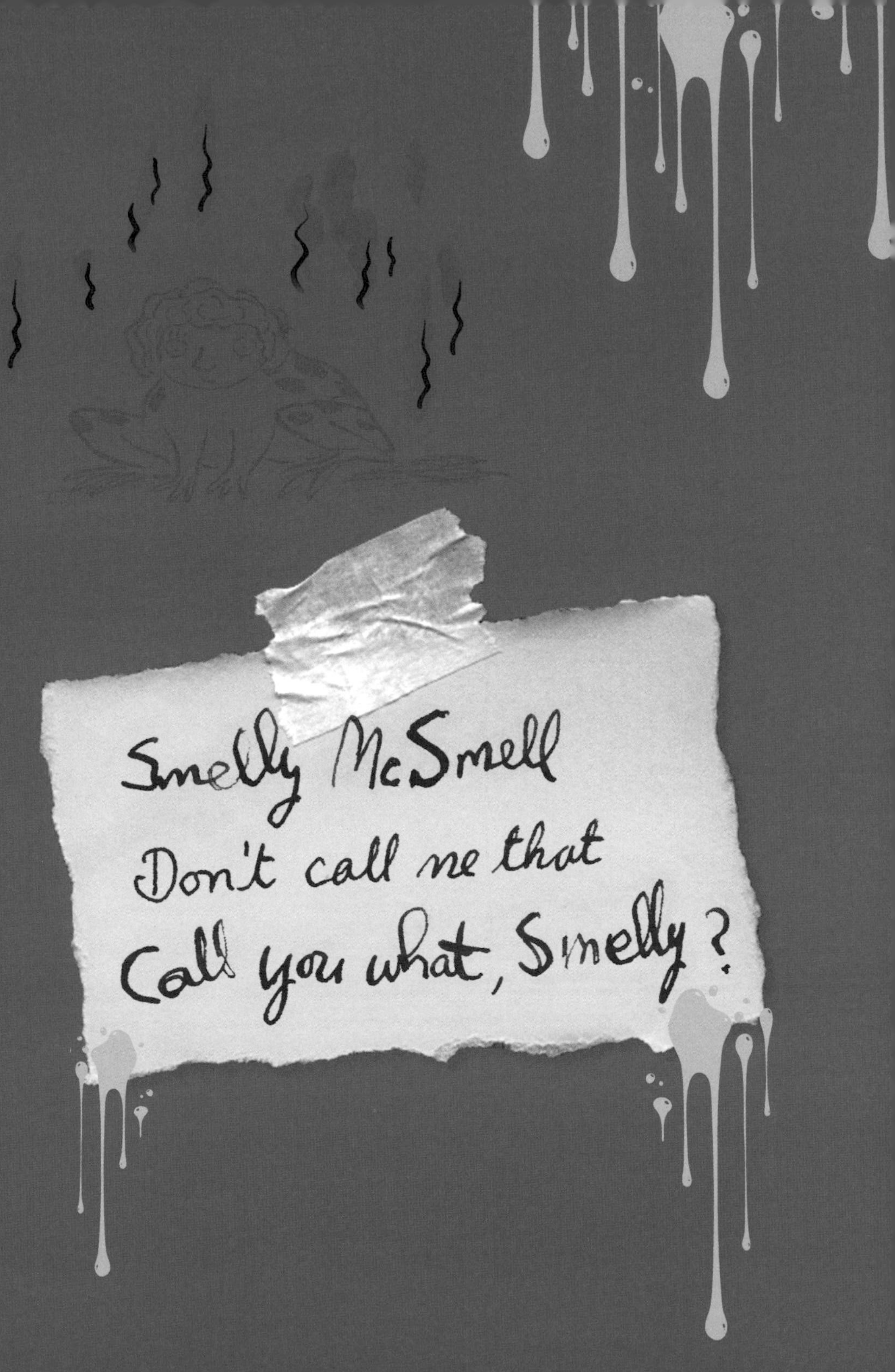
Smelly McSmell
Don't call me that
Call you what, Smelly?

HORRID HENRY'S
Author Visit

Horrid Henry woke up. He felt strange. He felt . . . happy. He felt . . . excited. But why?

Was it the weekend? No. Was it a day off school? No. Had Miss Battle-Axe been kidnapped by aliens and transported to another galaxy to slave in the salt mines? No (unfortunately).

So why was he feeling so excited on a school day?

And then Horrid Henry remembered.

Oh wow!! It was Book Week at Henry's school, and his favourite author in the whole world, TJ Fizz, the writer of the stupendous *Ghost Quest* and *Mad Machines* and *Skeleton Skunks* was coming to talk to his class. Henry had read every single one of TJ's brilliant books, even after lights out. Rude Ralph thought they were almost as good as Mutant Max comics. Horrid Henry thought they were even better.

Perfect Peter bounced into his room.

'Isn't it exciting, Henry?' said Perfect Peter. 'Our class is going to meet a real live author! Milksop Miles is coming today. He's the man who wrote *The Happy Nappy*. Do you think he'd sign my copy?'

Horrid Henry snorted.

The Happy Nappy! Only the dumbest book ever. All those giant nappies with names like Rappy Nappy and Zappy Nappy and Tappy Nappy dancing and prancing about. And then the truly horrible Gappy Nappy, who was always wailing, 'I'm leaking!'

Horrid Henry shuddered. He was amazed that Milksop Miles dared to show his face after writing such a boring book.

'Only a wormy toad like you could like such a stupid story,' said Henry.

'It's not stupid,' said Peter.

'Is too.'

'Is not. And he's bringing his guitar. Miss Lovely said so.'

'Big deal,' said Horrid Henry. '*We've* got TJ Fizz.'

Perfect Peter shuddered.

'Her books are too scary,' said Peter.

'That's 'cause you're a baby.'

'Mum!' shrieked Peter. 'Henry called me baby.'

'Telltale,' hissed Henry.

'Don't be horrid, Henry,' shouted Mum.

Horrid Henry sat in class with a huge carrier bag filled with all his TJ Fizz books. Everyone in the class had drawn book covers for *Ghost Quest* and *Ghouls' Jewels*, and written their own *Skeleton Skunk* story. Henry's of course was the best: *Skeleton Skunk meets Terminator Gladiator: May the smelliest fighter win!* He would give it to TJ Fizz if she paid him a million pounds.

Ten minutes to go. How could he live until it was time for her to arrive?

Miss Battle-Axe cleared her throat.

'Class, we have a very important guest coming. I know you're all very excited, but I will not tolerate anything but perfect behaviour today. Anyone who misbehaves will be sent out. Is that clear?' She glared at Henry.

Henry scowled back. Of course he would be perfect. TJ Fizz was coming!

'Has everyone thought of a good question to ask her? I'll write the best ones on the board,' continued Miss Battle-Axe.

'How much money do you make?' shouted Rude Ralph.

'How many TVs do you have?' shouted Horrid Henry.

'Do you like fudge?' shouted Greedy Graham.

'I said *good* questions,' snapped Miss Battle-Axe. 'Bert, what's your question for TJ Fizz?'

'I dunno,' said Beefy Bert.

Rumble.

Rumble.

Rumble.

Ooops. Henry's tummy was telling him it was snacktime.

It must be all the excitement. It was strictly forbidden to eat in class, but Henry was a master sneaker. He certainly wouldn't want his tummy to gurgle while TJ Fizz was talking.

Miss Battle-Axe was writing down Clever Clare's eight questions on the board.

Slowly, carefully, silently, Horrid Henry opened his lunchbox under the table. Slowly, carefully, silently, he eased open the bag of crisps.

Horrid Henry looked to the left.

Rude Ralph was waving his hand in the air.

Horrid Henry looked to the right.

Greedy Graham was drooling and opening a bag of sweets.

The coast was clear. Henry popped some Super Spicy Hedgehog crisps into his mouth.

MUNCH!

CRUNCH!

'C'mon Henry, give me some crisps,' whispered Rude Ralph.

'No,' hissed Horrid Henry. 'Eat your own.'

'I'm starving,' moaned Greedy Graham. 'Gimme a crisp.'

'No!' hissed Horrid Henry.

MUNCH!

CRUNCH!

YANK

Huh?

Miss Battle-Axe towered over him holding aloft his bag of crisps. Her red eyes were like two icy daggers.

'What did I tell you, Henry?' said Miss Battle-Axe. 'No bad behaviour would be tolerated. Go to Miss Lovely's class.'

'But . . . but . . . TJ Fizz is coming!' spluttered Horrid Henry. 'I was just–'

Miss Battle-Axe pointed to the door.

'Out!'

'NOOOOOOOOOO!' howled Henry.

Horrid Henry sat in a tiny chair at the back of Miss Lovely's room. Never had he suffered such torment. He tried to block his ears as Milksop Miles read his horrible book to Peter's class.

'Hello, Happy, Clappy and Yappy! Can you find the leak?'

'No,' said Happy.

'No,' said Clappy.

'No,'s aid Yappy.

'I can,' said Gappy Nappy.

AAAARRRRGGGGGHHH!

Horrid Henry gritted his teeth. He would go mad having to listen to this a moment longer.

He had to get out of here.

'All together now, let's sing the Happy Nappy song,' trilled Milksop Miles, whipping out his guitar.

'Yay!' cheered the infants.

No, groaned Horrid Henry.

Oh I'm a happy nappy,
a happy zappy nappy
I wrap up your bottom, snug and tight,
And keep you dry all through the night
Oh -

This was torture. No, this was worse than torture. How could he sit here listening to the horrible Happy

Nappy song knowing that just above him TJ Fizz was reading from one of her incredible books, passing round the famous skunk skeleton, and showing off her *Ghost Quest* drawings. He had to get back to his own class. He had to.

But how?

What if he joined in the singing? He could bellow:

Oh I'm a Soggy Nappy
A Smelly, Stinky Nappy–

Yes! That would certainly get him sent out the door straight to – the head. Not back to his class and TJ Fizz.

Horrid Henry closed his mouth. Rats.

Maybe there'd be an earthquake? A power failure? Where was a fire-drill when you needed one?

He could always pretend he needed the toilet. But then when he didn't come back they'd come looking for him.

Or maybe he could just sneak away? Why not? Henry got to his feet and began to slide towards the door, trying to be invisible.

Sneak Sneak Sn –

'Whooa, come back here, little boy,' shouted Milksop Miles, twanging his guitar. Henry froze. 'Our party is just starting. Now who knows the Happy Nappy dance?'

'I do,' said Perfect Peter.

'I do,' said Goody-Goody Gordon.

'We all do,' said Tidy Ted.

'Everyone on their feet,' said Milksop Miles. 'Ah-one ah-two, let's all do the Nappy Dance!'

'Nap nap nap nap nap nap nappy,' warbled Miles.

'Nap nap nap nap nap nap nappy,' warbled Peter's class, dancing away.

Desperate times call for desperate measures. Horrid Henry started dancing. Slowly, he tapped his way closer and closer and closer to the door and – freedom!

Horrid Henry reached for the door knob. Miss Lovely was busy dancing in the corner. Just a few more steps . . .

'Who's going to be my little helper while we act out the story?' beamed Miles. 'Who would like to play the Happy Nappy?'

'Me! Me!' squealed Miss Lovely's class.

Horrid Henry sank against the wall.

'Come on, don't be shy,' said Miles, pointing straight at Henry. 'Come on up and put on the magic happy nappy!' And he marched over and dangled an enormous blue nappy in front of Henry. It was over one metre wide and one metre high, with a hideous smiling face and big goggly eyes.

Horrid Henry took a step back. He felt faint. The giant nappy was looming above him. In a moment it would be over his head and he'd be trapped inside. His name would be mud – forever. Henry the nappy. Henry the giant nappy. Henry the giant happy nappy . . .

'**AAAARRRRGGGGGHHH!**'

screamed Horrid Henry. 'Get away from me!'

Milksop Miles stopped waving the gigantic nappy. 'Oh dear,' he said.

'Oh dear,' said Miss Lovely.

'Don't be scared,' said Miles.

Scared? Horrid Henry . . . scared? Of a giant nappy? Henry opened his mouth to scream.

And then he stopped.
What if . . . ?
'Help! Help! I'm
being attacked by
a nappy!' screeched
Henry. 'HELLLLLLLP!'
Milksop Miles looked at
Miss Lovely. Miss Lovely looked
at Milksop Miles.

'HELLLLLLLP! HELLLLLLLP!'

'Henry? Are you OK?' piped Perfect Peter.

'NOOOOOOOO!' wailed Horrid Henry,
cowering. 'I'm . . . I'm . . . nappy-phobic.'

'Never mind,' said Milksop Miles. 'You're not the
first boy who's been scared of a giant nappy.'

'I'm sure I'll be fine if I go back to my own class,'
gasped Horrid Henry.

Miss Lovely hesitated. Horrid Henry opened his
mouth to howl –
'Run along then,'
said Miss Lovely
quickly.

Horrid
Henry did not
wait to be asked
twice.

He raced out of Miss Lovely's class, then dashed upstairs to his own.

Skeleton Skunk here I come, thought Henry, bursting through the door.

There was the great and glorious TJ Fizz, just about to start reading a brand new chapter from her latest book, *Skeleton Stinkbomb*. Hallelujah, he was in time.

'Henry, what are you doing here?' hissed Miss Battle-Axe.

'Miss Lovely sent me back,' beamed Horrid Henry. 'And you did say we should be on our best behaviour today, so I did what I was told.'

Henry sat down as TJ began to read. The story was amazing.

Ahhh, sighed Horrid Henry happily, wasn't life grand?

Henry's Skeleton Skunk Story

Skeleton Skunk meets Terminator Gladiator. May the smelliest fighter win!!!!!!!

Chapter 1

Peeeeuuuwww. What a stink. What a smell. What a pong. The smelliest skunkiest fighter burst into the shop. He looked around at the terrified faces.

'All right, where is he?' snarled Skeleton Skunk. 'Where's that so-called Gladiator who calls himself Terminator? Because he is about to be terminated. Ahaha ha ha ha.'

'He ain't here, Skunk,' quivered the man behind the counter. 'Honest.'

'A likely story,' jeered Skeleton Skunk.

'No one's seen him,' said the man, shivering.

'That's 'cause he's a yellow-livered coward,' sneered Skeleton Skunk, 'and when I find him —'

'Who are you calling coward?' hissed a voice from the ceiling.

Skeleton Skunk looked up. There, swinging from the chandelier, was Terminator Gladiator.

Ooops, thought the Skunk. His bones rattled. Ooooops. Time for my top secret super-skunky plan . . .

by
Henry

HORRiD HENRY
and the Tv Remote

Horrid Henry pushed through the front door. Perfect Peter squeezed past him and ran inside.

'Hey!' screamed Horrid Henry, dashing after him. 'Get back here, worm.'

'Noooo!' squealed Perfect Peter, running as fast as his little legs would carry him.

Henry grabbed Peter's shirt, then hurtled past him into the sitting room. Yippee! He was going to get the comfy black chair first. Almost there, almost there, almost . . . and then Horrid Henry skidded on a sock and slipped. Peter pounded past and dived onto the comfy black chair. Panting and gasping, he snatched the remote control. Click!

'All together now! Who's a silly Billy?' trilled the world's most annoying goat.

'Billy!' sang out Perfect Peter.

NOOOOOOOOOOOOOO!

It had happened again. Just as Henry was looking forward to resting his weary bones on the comfy black chair after another long, hard, terrible day at school and watching *Rapper Zapper* and *Knight Fight*, Peter had somehow managed to nab the chair first. It was so unfair.

The rule in Henry's house was that whoever was sitting in the comfy black chair decided what to watch on TV. And there was Peter, smiling and singing along with Silly Billy, the revolting singing goat who thought he was a clown.

Henry's parents were so mean and horrible, they only had one teeny tiny telly in the whole, entire house. It was so minuscule Henry practically had to watch it using a magnifying glass. And so old you practically had to kick it to turn it on. Everyone else he knew had loads of TVs. Rude Ralph had five ginormous ones all to himself. At least, that's what Ralph said.

All too often there were at least two great programmes on at the same time. How was Henry supposed to choose between *Mutant Max* and

Terminator Gladiator? If only he could watch two TVs simultaneously, wouldn't life be wonderful?

Even worse, Mum, Dad, and Peter had their own smelly programmes *they* wanted to watch. And not great programmes like *Hog House* and *Gross Out*. Oh no. Mum and Dad liked watching . . . news. Documentaries. Opera. Perfect Peter liked nature programmes. And revolting baby programmes like *Daffy and her Dancing Daisies*. Uggghh! How did he end up in this family? When would his real parents, the King and Queen, come and fetch him and take him to the palace where he could watch whatever he wanted all day?

When he grew up and became King Henry the Horrible, he'd have three TVs in every room, including the bathrooms.

But until that happy day, he was stuck at home slugging it out with Peter. He *could* spend the afternoon watching *Silly Billy*, *Cooking Cuties*, and *Sammy the Snail*. Or . . .

Horrid Henry pounced and snatched the remote. CLICK!

'. . . and the black knight lowers his visor . . .'

'Give it to me,' shrieked Peter.

'No,' said Henry.

'But I've got the chair,' wailed Peter.

'So?' said Henry, waving the clicker at him. 'If you want the remote you'll have to come and get it.'

Peter hesitated. Henry dangled the remote just out of reach.

Perfect Peter slipped off the comfy black chair and grabbed for the remote. Horrid Henry ducked, swerved and jumped onto the empty chair.

'...And the knights are advancing towards one another, lances poised ...'

'MUUUUMMMM!' squealed Peter. 'Henry snatched the remote!'

'Did not!'

'Did too.'

'Did not, wibble pants.'

'Don't call me wibble pants,' cried Peter.

'Okay, pongy poo poo,' said Henry.

'Don't call me pongy poo poo,' shrieked Peter.

'Okay, wibble bibble,' said Horrid Henry.

'MUUUUUMMM!' wailed Peter. 'Henry's calling me names!'

'Henry! Stop being horrid,' shouted Mum.

'I'm just trying to watch TV in peace!' screamed Henry. 'Peter's annoying me.'

'Henry's annoying *me*,' whined Peter. 'He pushed me off the chair.'

'Liar,' said Henry. 'You fell off.'

'MUUUUMMMMMM!' screamed Peter.

Mum ran in, and grabbed the remote.

Click! The screen went black.

'I've had it with you boys fighting over the TV,' shouted Mum. 'No TV for the rest of the day.'

What?

Huh?

'But . . . but . . .' said Perfect Peter.

'But . . . but . . .' said Horrid Henry.

'No buts,' said Mum.

'It's not fair!' wailed Henry and Peter.

Horrid Henry paced up and down his room, whacking his teddy, Mr Kill, on the bedpost every time he walked past.

WHACK!

WHACK!

WHACK!

He had to find a way to make sure he watched the programmes *he* wanted to watch. He just had to. He'd have to get up at the crack of dawn. There was no other way.

Unless . . .

Unless . . .

And then Horrid Henry had a brilliant, spectacular idea. What an idiot he'd been. All those months he'd missed his fantastic shows . . . Well, never ever again.

Sneak.

Sneak.

Sneak.

It was the middle of the night. Horrid Henry crept down the stairs as quietly as he could and tiptoed into the sitting room, shutting the door behind him. There was the TV, grumbling in the corner. 'Why is no one watching me?' moaned the telly. 'C'mon, Henry.'

But for once Henry didn't listen. He had something much more important to do.

He crept to the comfy black chair and fumbled in the dark. Now, where was the remote? Aha! There it was. As usual, it had fallen between the seat cushion and the armrest. Henry grabbed it. Quick as a flash, he switched the TV over to the channel for *Rapper Zapper*, *Talent Tigers* and *Hog House*. Then he tiptoed to the toy cupboard and hid the remote control deep inside a bucket of multi-coloured bricks that no one had

played with for years.

Tee hee, thought Horrid Henry.

Why should he have to get up to grab the comfy black chair hours before his programmes started when he could have a lovely lie-in, saunter downstairs whenever he felt like it, and be master of the TV? Whoever was sitting in the chair could be in charge of the telly all they wanted. But without the TV remote, no one would be watching anything.

Perfect Peter stretched out on the comfy black chair. Hurrah. Serve Henry right for being so mean to him. Peter had got downstairs first. Now he could watch what *he* wanted all morning.

Peter reached for the remote control. It wasn't on the armrest. It wasn't on the headrest. Had it slipped between the armrest and the cushion? No. He felt round the back. No. He looked under the chair. Nothing. He looked behind the chair. Where was it?

Horrid Henry strolled into the sitting room. Peter clutched tightly onto the armrests in case Henry tried to push him off.

'I got the comfy black chair first,' said Peter.

'Okay,' said Horrid Henry, sitting down on the sofa. 'So let's watch something.'

Peter looked at Henry suspiciously.

'Where's the remote?' said Peter.

'I dunno,' said Horrid Henry. 'Where did you put it?'

'I didn't put it anywhere,' said Peter.

'You had it last,' said Henry.

'No I didn't,' said Peter.

'Did,' said Henry.

'Didn't,' said Peter.

Perfect Peter sat on the comfy black chair. Horrid Henry sat on the sofa.

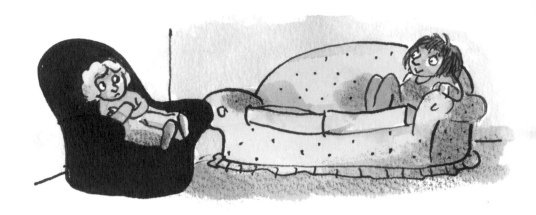

'Have you seen it anywhere?' said Peter.

'No,' said Henry. 'You'll just have to look for it, won't you?'

Peter eyed Henry warily.

'I'm waiting,' said Horrid Henry.

Perfect Peter didn't know what to do. If he got up from the chair to look for the remote Henry would jump into it and there was no way Henry would decide to watch *Cooking Cuties*, even though today they were showing how to make your own muesli.

On the other hand, there wasn't much point sitting in the chair if he didn't have the remote.

Henry sat.

Peter sat.

'You know, Peter, you can turn on the TV without the remote,' said Henry casually.

Peter brightened. 'You can?'

'Sure,' said Henry. 'You just press that big black button on the left.'

Peter stared suspiciously at the button. Henry must think he was an idiot. He could see Henry's plan from miles away. The moment Peter left the comfy black chair Henry would jump on it.

'You press it,' said Peter.

'Okay,' said Henry agreeably. He sauntered to the telly and pressed the 'on' button.

BOOM! CRASH! WALLOP!

'Des-troy! Des-troy!' bellowed Mutant Max.

'Go Mutants!' shouted Horrid Henry, bouncing up and down.

Perfect Peter sat frozen in the chair.

'But I want to watch *Sing-along with Susie!*' wailed Peter. 'She's teaching a song about raindrops and roses.'

'So find the remote,' said Horrid Henry.

'I can't,' said Peter.

'Tough,' said Horrid Henry. 'Pulverize! Destroy! Destroy!'

Tee hee.

What a fantastic day, sighed Horrid Henry happily. He'd watched every single one of *his* best programmes and Peter hadn't watched a single one of *his*. And now *Hog House* was on. Could life get any better?

Dad staggered into the sitting room. 'Ahh, a little relaxation in front of the telly,' sighed Dad. 'Henry, turn off that horrible programme. I want to watch the news.'

'Shhh!' said Horrid Henry. How dare Dad interrupt him?

'Henry . . .' said Dad.

'I can't,' said Horrid Henry. 'No remote.'

'What do you mean, no remote?' said Dad.

'It's gone,' said Henry.

'What do you mean, gone?' said Mum.

'Henry lost it,' said Peter.

'Didn't,' snapped Henry.

'Did,' said Peter.

'DIDN'T!' bellowed Henry. 'Now be quiet, I'm trying to watch.'

Mum marched over to the telly and switched it off. 'The TV stays off until the remote is found,' said Mum.

'But I didn't lose it!' wailed Peter.

'Neither did I,' said Horrid Henry. This wasn't a lie, as he *hadn't* lost it.

Rats. Maybe it was time for the TV remote to make a miraculous return . . .

Sneak.

        Sneak.

                Sneak.

Mum and Dad were in the kitchen. Perfect Peter was practising his cello.

Horrid Henry crept to the toy cupboard and opened it.

The bucket of bricks had gone.

Huh?

Henry searched frantically in the cupboard, hurling out jigsaw puzzles, board games, and half-empty paint bottles. The bricks were definitely gone.

Yikes. Horrid Henry felt a chill down his spine. He was dead. He was doomed.

Unless Mum had moved the bricks somewhere. Of course. Phew. He wasn't dead yet.

Mum walked into the sitting room.

'Mum,' said Henry casually, 'I wanted to build a castle with those old bricks but when I went to get them from the cupboard they'd gone.'

Mum stared at him. 'You haven't played with those bricks in years, Henry. I had a good clear out of all the baby toys today and gave them to the charity shop.'

Charity shop? Charity shop? That meant the remote was gone for **good**. He would be in trouble. Big big trouble. He was doomed . . . NOT!

Without the clicker, the TV would be useless. Mum and Dad would *have* to buy a new one. Yes! A bigger, better fantastic one with twenty-five surround-sound speakers and a mega-whopper 10-foot super-sized screen!

'You know, Mum, we wouldn't have any arguments if we all had our *own* TVs,' said Henry. Yes! In fact, if he had two in his bedroom, and a third one spare in case one of them ever broke, he'd never argue about the telly again.

Mum sighed. 'Just find the remote,' she said. 'It must be here somewhere.'

'But our TV is so old,' said Henry.

'It's fine,' said Dad.

'It's horrible,' said Henry.

'We'll see,' said Mum.

New TV here I come, thought Horrid Henry happily.

Mum sat down on the sofa and opened her book.

Dad sat down on the sofa and opened his book.

Peter sat down on the sofa and opened his book.

'You know,' said Mum, 'it's lovely and peaceful without the telly.'

'Yes,' said Dad.

'No squabbling,' said Mum.

'No screaming,' said Dad.

'Loads of time to read good books,' said Mum.

They smiled at each other.

'I think we should be a telly-free home from now on,' said Dad.

'Me too,' said Mum.

'That's a great idea,' said Perfect Peter. 'More time to do homework.'

'What??' screamed Horrid Henry. He thought his heart would stop. No TV? No TV?

'NOOOOOOOOOOO!
NOOOOOOOOOOO!
NOOOOOOOOOOOO!'

BANG! ZAP! KER-POW!

'Go mutants!' yelped Horrid Henry, bouncing up and down in the comfy black chair.

Mum and Dad had resisted buying a new telly for two long hard horrible weeks. Finally they'd given in. Of course they hadn't bought a big mega-whopper super-duper telly. Oh no. They'd bought the teeniest, tiniest, titchiest telly they could.

Still. It was a *bit* bigger than the old one. And the remote could always go missing again . . .

Ten reasons why watching TV is better than reading

1. Holding a book is very tiring

2. Turning pages is very tiring

3. Moving your eyes from left to right is very tiring

4. You can eat crisps while watching TV

5. You can chat while watching TV

6. You can do your homework while watching TV

7. You can play computer games and watch TV at the same time

8. You can dance while watching TV

9. There are great programmes on TV, like *Hog House* and *Knight Fight* and *Terminator Gladiator*

10. No one ever tests you about what you watched on TV

Of all the worms in the world,
you're the wormiest worm.

Am not.

Am too.

HORRID HENRY'S
School Election

Yack yack yack yack yack.

Horrid Henry's legs ached. His head ached. His bottom really ached. How much longer would he have to sit on this hard wooden floor and listen to Mrs Oddbod witter on about hanging up coats and no running in the corridors and walking down staircases on the right-hand side? Why were school assemblies so boring? If he were head, assemblies would be about the best TV programmes, competitions for gruesome grub recipes and speed-eating contests.

Yack. Yack. Yack. Yack. Yack.

Zoom . . . Zoom . . . Squawk! Horrid Henry's hawk swooped and scooped up Mrs Oddbod in his fearsome beak.

Chomp.

Chomp.

Ch– Wait a minute. What was she saying?

'School elections will be held next week,' said Mrs Oddbod. 'For the first time ever you'll be electing a School Council President. Now I want everyone to think of someone they believe would make an outstanding President. Someone who will make important decisions which will affect everyone, someone worthy of this high office, someone who will represent this school . . .'

Horrid Henry snorted. School elections? Phooey! Who'd want to be School Council President? All that responsibility . . . all that power . . . all that glory . . . Wait. What was he thinking? Who wouldn't want to be?

Imagine, being President! He'd be king, emperor, Lord High Master of the Universe! He'd make Mrs

Oddbod walk the plank. He'd send Miss Battle-Axe to be a galley slave. He'd make playtime last for five hours. He'd ban all salad and vegetables from school dinners and just serve sweets! And Fizzywizz drinks!

And everyone would have to bow down to him as they entered the school! And give him chocolate every day.

President Henry. His Honour, President Henry. It had a nice ring. So did King Henry. Emperor Henry would be even better though. He'd change his title as soon as he got the throne.

And all he had to do was win the election.

Shout!

Shriek!

'Silence!' screeched Mrs Oddbod. 'Any more noise and playtime will be cancelled!'

Huumph, that was one thing that would never happen when he was School President. In fact, he'd make it a rule that anyone who put their hand up in class would get sent to him for punishment. There'd only be shouting out in *his* school.

'Put up your hand if you wish to nominate someone,' said Mrs Oddbod.

Sour Susan's hand shot up. 'I nominate Margaret,' she said.

'I accept!' yelled Margaret, preening.

Horrid Henry choked. Margaret? Bossyboots Margaret *President*? She'd be a disaster, a horrible, grumpy, grouchy, moody disaster. Henry would never hear the end of it. Her head would swell so much it would burst. She'd be swaggering all over the place, ordering everyone around, boasting, bossing, showing off . . .

Horrid Henry's hand shot up. 'I nominate . . . me!' he shrieked.

'You?' said Mrs Oddbod coldly.

'Me,' said Horrid Henry.

'I second it,' shouted Rude Ralph.

Henry beamed at Ralph. He'd make Ralph his Grand Vizier. Or maybe Lord High Executioner. 'Any more nominations?' said Mrs Oddbod.

She looked unhappy. 'Come on, Bert, what would you do to improve the school?'

'I dunno,' said Bert.

'Clare?' said Mrs Oddbod.

'More fractions!' said Clare.

Horrid Henry caught Ralph's eye.

'Boo!' yelled Ralph. 'Down with Clare!'

'Yeah, boo!' yelled Dizzy Dave.

'Boo!' hissed Horrid Henry.

'Last chance to nominate anyone else,' said Mrs Oddbod desperately.

Silence.

'All right,' said Mrs Oddbod, 'you have two candidates for President. Posters can be displayed from tomorrow. Speeches the day after tomorrow. Good luck to both candidates.'

Horrid Henry glared at Moody Margaret.

Moody Margaret glared at Horrid Henry.

I'll beat that grumpface frog if it's the last thing I do, thought Horrid Henry.

I'll beat that pongy pants pimple if it's the last thing I do, thought Moody Margaret.

'Vote Margaret! Margaret for President!' trilled Sour Susan the next day, as she and Margaret handed out leaflets during playtime.

'Ha ha Henry, I'm going to win, and you're not!' chanted Margaret, sticking out her tongue.

'Yeah Henry, Margaret's going to win,' said Sour Susan.

'Oh yeah?' said Henry. Wait till she saw his fantastic campaign posters with the big picture of King Henry the Horrible.

'Yeah.'

'We'll see about that,' said Horrid Henry.

He'd better start campaigning at once. Now, whose votes could he count on?

Ralph's for sure. And, uh
. . . um . . . uhmmmm . . .
Ralph.

Toby *might* vote for
him but he'd probably
have to beg. Hmmm. Two
votes were not enough
to win. He'd have to get
more support. Well, no
time like the present to
remind everyone what
a great guy he was.

Zippy Zoe zipped
past. Horrid Henry smiled at her.
Zoe stopped dead.

'Why are you smiling at me, Henry?' said Zippy
Zoe. She checked to see if she'd come to
school wearing pyjamas or if her
jumper had a big hole.

'Just because it's so nice to
see you,' said Horrid Henry.
'Will you vote for me for
President?'

Zoe stared at him.
'Margaret gave me a pencil
with her name on it,' said Zoe.

'And a sticker. What will *you* give me?'

Give? Give? Horrid Henry liked getting. He did not like giving. So Margaret was bribing people, was she? Well, two could play at that game. He'd bring loads of sweets into school tomorrow and hand them out to everyone who promised to vote for him. That would guarantee victory!

And he'd make sure that everyone had to give him sweets after he'd won.

Anxious Andrew walked by wearing a 'Margaret for President' sticker.

'Oooh, Andrew, I wouldn't vote for her,' said Henry. 'Do you know what she's planning to do?' Henry whispered in Andrew's ear. Andrew gasped.

'No,' said Andrew.

'Yes,' said Henry. 'And ban crisps, too. You know what an old bossyboots Margaret is.'

Henry handed him a leaflet.

Andrew looked uncertain.

'Vote for me and I'll make you Vice-Chairman of the Presidential Snacks Sub-committee.'

'Oooh,' said Andrew.

Henry promised the same job to Dizzy Dave, Jolly Josh, and Weepy William.

He promised Needy Neil his mum could sit with him in class. He promised Singing Soraya she could sing every day in assembly. He promised Greedy Graham there'd be ice cream every day for lunch.

The election is in the bag, thought Horrid Henry gleefully. He fingered the magic marker in his pocket. Tee hee. Just wait till Margaret saw how he was planning to graffiti her poster! And wasn't it lucky it was impossible to graffiti his name or change it to something rude. Shame, thought Horrid Henry, that Peter wasn't running for President. If you crossed out the 't' and the 'r' you'd get 'Vote for Pee'.

Vote for Pe~~ter~~

Horrid Henry strolled over to the wall where the campaign posters were displayed.

Huh?

What?

A terrible sight met his eyes. His 'Vote for Henry' posters had been defaced. Instead of his crowned head, a horrible picture of a chicken's head had been glued on top of his body. And the 'ry' of his name had been crossed out.

Beneath it was written:

Cluck cluck yuck! Vote for a Hen? No way!

146

What a dirty trick, thought Horrid Henry
indignantly. How dare Margaret deface his posters!
Just because he'd handed out leaflets showing Margaret
with a frog's face. Margaret *was* a frog-face. The school
needed to know the truth about her.

Well, no more Mr Nice Guy. This was war.

Moody Margaret entered the playground. A terrible
sight met her eyes. All her 'Vote Margaret' posters had
been defaced. Huge beards and moustaches had been
drawn on every one. Beneath the picture, instead of
'Be on target! Vote Margaret!' the words now read:

The next poster read:

VoTe Margrunt
oink, oink, oink

How dare Henry graffiti over her posters! I'll get you Henry, thought Margaret. Just wait until tomorrow.

The next day was campaign speech day. Horrid Henry sat on the stage with Moody Margaret in front of the entire school. He was armed and ready. Margaret

148

would be blasted from the race. As Margaret rose to speak, Henry made a horrible, gagging face.

'We face a great danger,' said Moody Margaret. 'Do you want a leader like me? Or a loser like Henry? Do you want someone who will make you proud of this school? Or someone like Henry who will make you ashamed? I will be the best President ever. I'm already Captain of the Football Team. I know how to tell people what to do. This school will be heaven with me in charge. Remember, a vote for me will brighten every school day.'

'Go Margaret!' yelled Sour Susan as Margaret sat down.

Horrid Henry rose to speak.

'When I'm President,' said Horrid Henry, 'I promise a Goo-Shooter day! I promise a Gross-Out day! With my best friend Marvin the Maniac presenting the prize. School will start at lunchtime, and end after playtime. Gobble and Go will run the school cafeteria. I promise no homework! I promise skateboarding in the hall! I promise ice cream! And sweets!

'If you vote for Margaret, you'll get a dictator. And how do I know this? Because I have discovered her top-secret plans!' Horrid Henry pulled out a piece of paper covered in writing and showed it to the hall. 'Just listen to what she wrote:

Margaret's Top Secret Plans for when I am President

The school day is too short. School will end at 6.00 when I'm in charge

I look at my school lunch and I think, 'Why is there a desert on my plate when there should be more vegetables?' All sweets and desserts will be banned

There isn't enough homework at this School. Five hours of homework every night

Get rid of school holidays. Who needs them?

Ban chips!

Ban football!

Ban playtime!

'I never wrote that!' screeched Margaret.

'She would say that, wouldn't she?' said Henry smoothly. 'But the voters need to know the truth.'

'He's lying!' shouted Margaret.

'Don't be fooled, everyone! Margaret will ban sweets! Margaret will ban crisps! Margaret will make you do lots more homework. Margaret wants to have school seven days a week.

'So vote Henry if you want to stop this evil fiend! Vote Henry for loads of sweets! Vote Henry for loads of fun! Vote Henry for President!'

'Henry! Henry! Henry!' shouted Ralph, as Henry sat down to rapturous applause.

He'd done it! He'd won! And by a landslide. Yes!! He was President Lord High Master of the Universe! Just wait till he started bossing everyone around! Margaret had been defeated – at last!

Mrs Oddbod glared at Henry as they sat in her office after the results had been announced. She looked grey.

'As President, you will call the school council

meeting to order. You will organise the toilet tidy rota. You will lead the litter collection every playtime.'

Horrid Henry's knees felt weak.

Toilet . . . tidy . . . rota? Litter? What?? That was his job? That's why he'd schemed and bribed and fought and campaigned and given away all those sweets?

Where was his throne? His title? His power? NOOO!

'I resign!' said Horrid Henry.

Rotas

School Toilet Tidy rota

Monday	Peter
Tuesday	Margaret
Wednesday	Peter
Thursday	Margaret
Friday	Peter

School Litter Patrol

Monday	Margaret and Peter
Tuesday	Peter and Margaret
Wednesday	Margaret and Peter
Thursday	Peter and Margaret
Friday	Margaret and Peter

MOODY MARGARET'S
School

'**P**ay attention, Susan,' shrieked Moody Margaret, 'or you'll go straight to the head.'

'I *am* paying attention,' said Sour Susan.

'This is boring,' said Horrid Henry. 'I want to play pirates.'

'Silence,' said Moody Margaret, whacking her ruler on the table.

'I want to be the teacher,' said Susan.

'No,' said Margaret.

'*I'll* be the teacher,' said Horrid Henry. He'd send the class straight out for play-time, and tell them to run for their lives.

'Are you out of your mind?' snapped Margaret.

'Can I be the teacher?' asked Perfect Peter.

'NO!' shouted Margaret, Susan, and Henry.

'Why can't I be the head?' said Susan sourly.

'Because,' said Margaret.

''cause why?' said Susan.

''cause *I'm* the head.'

'But you're the head *and* the teacher,' said Susan. 'It's not fair.'

'It is too fair, 'cause you'd make a terrible head,' said Margaret.

'Wouldn't!'

'Would!'

'I think we should take turns being head,' said Susan.

'That,' said Margaret, 'is the dumbest idea I've ever heard. Do you see Mrs Oddbod taking *turns* being head? I don't think so.'

Margaret's class grumbled mutinously on the carpet inside the Secret Club tent.

'Class, I will now take the register,' intoned Margaret. 'Susan?'

'Here.'

'Peter?'

'Here.'

'Henry?'

'In the toilet.'

Margaret scowled.

'We'll try that again. Henry?'

'Flushed away.'

'Last chance,' said Margaret severely. 'Henry?'

'Dead.'

Margaret made a big cross in her register.
'I will deal with you
later.'

'No one made *you*
the big boss,' muttered
Horrid Henry.

'It's *my* house and
we'll play what I want,'
said Moody Margaret. 'And I
want to play school.'

Horrid Henry scowled. Whenever Margaret came
to *his* house she was the guest and he had to play what
she wanted. But whenever Henry went to her house
Margaret was the boss 'cause it was *her* house. Ugggh.
Why oh why did he have to live next door to Moody
Margaret?

Mum had important work to do, and needed total
peace and quiet, so Henry and Peter had been dumped
at Margaret's. Henry had begged to go to Ralph's,
but Ralph was visiting his grandparents. Now he was
trapped all day with a horrible, moody old grouch.
Wasn't it bad enough being with Miss Battle-Axe all
week without having to spend his whole precious
Saturday stuck at Margaret's? And, even worse, playing
school?

'Come on, let's play pirates,' said Henry. 'I'm Captain Hook. Peter, walk the plank!'

'No,' said Margaret. 'I don't want to.'

'But I'm the guest,' protested Henry.

'So?' said Margaret. 'This is *my* house and we play by *my* rules.'

'Yeah, Henry,' said Sour Susan.

'And I love playing school,' said Perfect Peter. 'It's such fun doing sums.'

Grrr. If only Henry could just go home. 'I want a good report,' Mum had said, 'or you won't be going to Dave's bowling party tonight. It's very kind of Margaret and her mum to have you boys over to play.'

'But I don't want to go to Margaret's!' howled Henry. 'I want to stay home and watch TV!'

'N-O spells no,' said Mum, and sent him kicking and screaming next door. 'You can come home at five o'clock to get ready for Dave's party and not a minute before.'

Horrid Henry gazed longingly over the wall. His house looked so inviting. There was his bedroom window, twinkling at him. And his lonesome telly, stuck all by itself in the sitting room, just begging him to come over and switch it on. And all his wonderful toys, just waiting to be played

with. Funny, thought Horrid Henry, his toys seemed so boring when he was in his room. But now that he was trapped at Margaret's, there was so much he longed to do at home.

Wait. He could hide out in his fort until five. Yes! Then he'd stroll into his house as if he'd been at Margaret's all day. But then Margaret's mum would be sure to call his mum to say that Henry had vanished and Henry would get into trouble. Big, big trouble. Big, big, banned from Dave's party trouble.

Or, he'd pretend to be sick. Margaret's mum was such an old fusspot she'd be sure to send him home immediately. Yippee. He was a genius. This would be easy. A few loud coughs, a few dramatic clutches at his stomach, a dash to the loo, and he'd be sent straight home and . . . oops. He'd be put to bed. No party.

No pizza. No bowling. And what was the point of pretending to be sick at the *weekend*? He was trapped.

Moody Margaret whacked her ruler on the table.

'I want everyone to write a story,' said Margaret.

Write a story! Boy would Horrid Henry write a story. He seized a piece of paper and a pencil and scribbled away.

'Who'd like to read their story to the class?' said Margaret.

'I will,' said Henry.

Once upon a time there was a moody old grouch named Margaret. Margaret had been born a frog but an ugly wizard cursed the frog and turned it into Margaret.

'That's enough, Henry,' snapped Margaret. Henry ignored her.

'Ribbet ribbet,' said Margaret Frog. 'Ribbet ribbet ribbet.' Everyone in the kingdom tried to get rid of this horrible croaking moody monster. But she smelled so awful that no one could get near her. And then one day a hero named Heroic Henry came, and he held his nose, grabbed the Margaret Monster and hurled her into outer space where she exploded and was never seen again.   THE END

Susan giggled. Margaret glared.

'Fail,' said Margaret.

'Why?' said Horrid Henry innocently.

''Cause,' said Margaret. 'I'm the teacher and I say it was boring.'

'Did you think my story was boring, Peter?' demanded Henry.

Peter looked nervous.

'Did you?' said Margaret.

'Well, uhm, uhmm, I think mine is better,' said Peter.

Once upon a time there was a tea towel named Terry. He was a very sad tea towel because he didn't have any dishes to dry. One day he found a lot of wet

dishes. Swish swish swish, they were dry in no time. 'Yippee', said Terry the Tea Towel, 'I wonder when—'

'Boring!' shouted Horrid Henry.

'Excellent, Peter,' said Moody Margaret. '*Much* better than Henry's.'

Susan read out a story about her cat.

My cat Kitty Kat is a big fat cat. She says meow. One day Kitty Kat met a dog. Meow, said Kitty Kat. Woof woof, said the dog. Kitty Kat ran away. So did the dog. The end.

'OK class, here are your marks,' said Margaret. 'Peter came first.'

'Yay!' said Perfect Peter.

'*What?*' said Susan. 'My story was way better than his.'

'Susan came second, Henry came ninth.'

'How can I be ninth if there are only three people in the class?' demanded Horrid Henry.

''Cause that's how bad your story was,' said Margaret. 'Now, I've done some worksheets for you. No talking or there'll be no break.'

'Goody,' said Perfect Peter. 'I love worksheets. Are there lots of hard spelling words to learn?'

Horrid Henry had had enough. It was time to turn into Heroic Henry and destroy this horrible hag.

Henry crumpled up his worksheet and stood up.

'I've just been pretending to be a student,' shouted Henry. 'In fact, I'm a school inspector. And I'm shutting your school down. It's a disgrace.'

Margaret gasped.

'You're a moody old grouch and you're a terrible teacher,' said the inspector.

'I am not,' said Margaret.

'She is not,' said Susan.

'Silence when the inspector is speaking! You're the worst teacher I've ever seen. Imagine marking a stupid story about a tea towel higher than a fantastic tale about a wicked wizard.'

'I'm the head,' said Margaret. 'You can't boss me around.'

'I'm the inspector,' said Henry. 'I can boss *everyone* around.'

'Wrong, Henry,' said Margaret, 'because I'm the *chief* school inspector, and I'm inspecting *you*.'

'Oh no you're not,' said Henry.

'Oh yes I am,' said Margaret.

'An inspector can't be a head *and* a teacher, so there,' said Henry.

'Oh yes I can,' said Margaret.

'No you can't, 'cause I'm king and I send you to the Tower!' shrieked King Henry the Horrible.

'I'm the empress!' screamed Margaret. 'Go to jail.'

'I'm king of the universe, and I send you to the snakepit,' shrieked Henry.

'I'm queen of the universe and I'm going to chop off your head!'

'Not if I chop off yours first!' shrieked the king, yanking on the queen's hair.

The queen screamed and kicked the king.

The king screamed and kicked the queen.

'MUM!' screamed Margaret.

Margaret's mother rushed into the Secret Club tent.

'What's wrong with my little snugglechops?' said Margaret's mum.

'Henry's not playing my game,' said Margaret. 'And he kicked me.'

'She kicked me first,' said Henry.

'If you children can't play nicely I'll have to send you all home,' said Margaret's mother severely.

'No!' said Peter.

Send him . . . home. Yes! Henry would make Margaret scream until the walls fell down. He would tell Margaret's mum her house smelled of poo. He could . . . he would . . .

But if Henry was sent home for being horrid,

Mum and Dad would be furious. There'd be no pizza and bowling party for sure.

Unless . . . unless . . . It was risky.

It was dangerous. It could go horribly, horribly wrong. But desperate times call for desperate measures.

'Need a drink,' said Henry, and ran out of the tent before Margaret could stop him.

Henry went into the kitchen to find Margaret's mum.

'I'm worried about Margaret, I think she's getting sick,' said Henry.

'My little Maggie-muffin?' gasped Margaret's mum.

'She's being very strange,' said Henry sadly. 'She said she's the queen of the world and she would cut off my head.'

'Margaret would *never* say such a thing,' said her Mum. 'She always plays beautifully. I've never seen a child so good at sharing.'

Horrid Henry nodded. 'I know. It must be 'cause she's sick. Maybe she caught something from Peter.'

'Has Peter been ill?' said Margaret's mum. She looked pale.

'Oh yeah,' lied Henry. 'He's been throwing up,

and – and – well, it's been awful. But I'm sure he's not
very contagious.'

'Throwing up?' said Margaret's mum weakly.

'And diarrhoea,' said Henry. 'Loads and loads.'

Margaret's mother looked ashen.

'Diarrhoea?'

'But he's much better now,' said Henry. 'He's only
run to the loo five times since we've been here.'

Margaret's mother looked faint. 'My little Margaret
is so delicate . . . I can't risk . . . ' she gasped. 'I think
you and Peter had better go home straight away.
Margaret! Margaret! Come in at once,' she shouted.

Horrid Henry did not wait to be told twice. School
was out!

Ahhhh, thought Horrid Henry happily, reaching for the TV clicker, this was the life. Margaret had been sent to bed. He and Peter had been sent home. There was enough time to watch *Marvin the Maniac* and *Terminator Gladiator* before Dave's party.

'I can't help it that Margaret wasn't feeling well, Mum,' said Horrid Henry.

'I just hope I haven't caught anything from *her*.' Honestly.

Mum was so selfish.

School Reports

This so-called teacher should be locked in a dungeon with loads of rats for company! And then she should be dropped into a snakepit. She is a tyrant. She is a moody old grouch. She is an idiot. Imagine preferring a story about a tea towel to a brilliant adventure about a superhero, Heroic Henry, battling against a horrible hag, the Margaret Monster. That alone is grounds for imprisonment!!! Margaret is a menace. Never, ever go anywhere near her class.

Henry

This boy is so horrid he needs to go straight to jail. I think a few years on bread and water is the only solution. His so-called story was the worst I have ever read. A dreadful student. He should be made to wear a dunce's cap and a warning sign, 'Beware: horrid boy. Do not feed.'

Margaret

You're the biggest worm, Henry

Just for that, worm, you're
fired from the Purple Hand
forever.

HORRID HENRY'S
Bedtime

'**W**hat are you doing in my room?'
screamed Horrid Henry.

How dare Peter come into his bedroom? Couldn't he read the sign?

SMELLY TOAD BROTHERS
KEEP OUT

'Looking for my blue pencil,' said Peter. He stared at the piles of comics and sweet wrappers and dirty clothes and toys littering the floor, the bed and the chest of drawers.

'Well it's not in here, so get out,' hissed Henry. So what if he'd pinched Peter's pencil? He'd had a huge bit of sky to colour in. 'And don't you dare touch anything.'

'You should be in your pyjamas,' said Perfect Peter. '*I* am.'

'Whoopee for you,' said Horrid Henry. 'Now get lost.'

Peter wrinkled his nose. 'Your room stinks.'

'That's 'cause you're in it, smelly.'

'Mum!' screamed Peter. 'Henry called me smelly.'

'Stop being horrid, Henry!' screamed Mum.

'Smelly, smelly, smelly,' jeered Henry. 'Smelly, smelly, smelly.'

'MUM!' wailed Peter. 'He did it again.'

'Tattle-tale!'

'Meanie!'

'Poo breath!'

'Stinky!'

'Mega-stink!'

Perfect Peter paused. He'd run out of bad names to call Henry.

Horrid Henry had not run out of bad names to call Peter.

'Baby! Nappy-Face! Ugg! Worm! Toad! Ugly! Pongy-Pants! Duke of Poop!'

'MUUUUMMMMM!' screamed Peter.

Mum and Dad burst into the room.

'That's enough!' shouted Mum. She looked at her watch. 'It's eight o'clock. Why aren't you in your pyjamas, Henry? Bedtime, both of you.'

'Hurray,' said Perfect Peter. 'I love going to bed.'

What? Bedtime?

The hateful, horrible word thudded round the room.

'NO!' shrieked Horrid Henry. It couldn't be
bedtime *already*.

'I'm sorry I've been naughty, Mum,' said Perfect
Peter. 'I was so busy doing tomorrow night's
homework I didn't notice the time.'

'Don't worry,' said Mum, smiling.

Then she scowled at Henry.

'Why aren't you ready for bed? Peter is.'

'I'm not tired!' screamed Henry. 'I don't want to
go to bed.'

'I do,' said Perfect Peter.

Mum sighed.

Dad sighed.

'Henry, you know the rules,' said Dad. 'In bed at eight. Lights out at eight-thirty.'

'It's not fair!' screamed Henry. 'No one goes to bed at eight.' Except for Lazy Linda, who was asleep at seven, no one went to bed so early. Toby went to bed at nine. Margaret went to bed at nine-thirty (so she said, though Henry wasn't sure he believed her). Ralph didn't even have a bedtime.

But no. His mean, horrible parents hated him so much they shoved him into bed when everyone else was still rampaging and having fun.

Bedtime. Bleeech. What a hateful, horrible, evil word. A word, thought Horrid Henry bitterly, as horrid as *cabbage*, *prison*, *Peter*, and *school*. When he was King any parent who dared to tell their kids to go to bed would be sent to bed themselves at five o'clock forever.

AAARRGGHH! Why did he have to go to bed? He had **TV to watch!** Computer games to play! Comics to read!

'But I'm not tired!' howled Henry.

'We're growing boys, Henry, and we need our rest,' said Perfect Peter. 'Early to bed, early to rise, makes a boy healthy, wealthy—'

'Shut up, Peter,' snarled Henry, pouncing. He was Hurricane Henry, blowing away the last remaining human.

'AIEEEEEEE!' screeched Peter.

'Stop being horrid, Henry!' yelled Mum.

'Go to bed this minute!' yelled Dad.

'NO!' shouted Henry.

'Yes!' shouted Mum.

His parents didn't have a bedtime. Oh no. They could stay up as late as they liked. It was so unfair.

'I'm not tired and I won't go to bed!' shrieked Henry. He lay on the floor, kicking and screaming.

Mum looked at Dad.

Dad looked at Mum.

'My turn to put Peter to bed,' shouted Dad, trying

to be heard over Henry's howls.

'*My* turn to put Peter to bed,' shouted Mum.
'I got Henry into bed last night.'

'Uhh uhh . . . are you sure?' screeched Dad.
He looked pale.

'YES!' shouted Mum. 'How
could I forget? Come on, Peter,
what do you want for your
bedtime story?'

'*Sammy the Snuggly
Snail*,' said Perfect Peter,
scampering off to bed.
'*Slimy the Slug* was too
scary.'

Mum scampered
after him.

'I WON'T GO TO BED! I want to watch
Cannibal Cook!' howled Henry.

Cannibal Cook was
this brilliant new TV
show where chefs
competed to see who
could cook the most
revolting meals. Last
time *Gourmet Greg* had
whipped up lizard eyes

in custard. Tonight *Nibbling Nigel* was fighting back with jellied worm soufflé.

'It's so *boring* being in bed,' screamed Henry.

'I don't care,' said Dad firmly. 'It's bedtime – now!'

Strange, thought Horrid Henry as he paused for breath between shrieks. At night, he never wanted to get into bed, but in the morning he never wanted to get out of it.

But now was not the time for philosophy. He had important work to do if he was going to delay the evil moment as long as he possibly could.

'Just let me finish my drawing.'

'No,' said Dad.

'Please.'

'N-o spells no,' said Dad.

'It's my homework,' lied Henry.

'Oh all right,' said Dad. 'Hurry up.'

Henry drew a dragon very slowly.

Dad looked at the clock. It was 8:35.

'Come on, Henry,' said Dad. He stood there tapping his foot.

Henry coloured in the
dragon very very slowly.

'Henry . . .' said Dad.

Henry drew the dragon's
cave very very very slowly.

'That's enough, Henry,'
said Dad. 'Now brush your
teeth and get into bed.'

'I've already brushed my
teeth,' said Henry.

'Henry . . .' said Dad.

'Oh all right,' said Horrid Henry. After all, he held
the record for the world's
slowest tooth brusher.

Slowly Henry brushed his front teeth. Slowly
Henry brushed his back teeth.

Brush.

    Brush.

Brush.

    Brush.

Brush.

Dad stood in the
doorway glaring.

'Hurry up!'

'But Dad,' said Horrid Henry indignantly. 'Do
you want me to get fillings?'

'Bed. Now.'

'You'll be sorry when my teeth all fall out because you stopped me from brushing them,' said Henry.

Dad sighed. He'd been sighing a lot lately.

Horrid Henry stood at the bottom of the stairs.

'I can't walk – I'm too floppy,' said Horrid Henry.

'So crawl,' said Dad.

'My legs are too wobbly,' moaned Horrid Henry.

'So wobble,' said Dad.

Delicious smells floated up from the kitchen. Mum was cooking spaghetti with meatballs. Only his favourite dinner. How could he be expected to go to bed with all that good cooking going on downstairs?

'I'm hungry,' said Henry.

'The kitchen is closed,' said Dad.

'I'm thirsty,' said Henry.

'I'll bring you water once you're in bed.'

Dad was being tough tonight, thought Horrid Henry. But not too tough for me.

And then suddenly Horrid Henry had an idea. A brilliant, spectacular idea. True, his parents could make him go to bed – eventually. But they couldn't make him *stay* there, could they?

Horrid Henry yawned loudly.

'I guess I am quite tired, Dad,' said Horrid Henry. 'Will you tuck me in?'

'I said, get into – what did you say?'

'I'm ready for bed now,' said Henry.

Horrid Henry walked upstairs to his bedroom.

Horrid Henry got into his pyjamas and jumped into bed.

'Goodnight Dad,' said Henry.

'Goodnight Henry,' said Dad, tucking him in. 'Sleep well,' he added, leaving the room with a big, beaming smile on his face.

Horrid Henry leapt out of bed. Quickly he gathered up some blankets and a pile of dirty clothes from the floor. Then he stuffed blanket and clothes under the duvet. Perfect, thought Horrid Henry.

Anyone glancing in would think he was snuggled up in bed fast asleep under the covers.

Tee hee, thought Horrid Henry.

He tiptoed to the door.

The coast was clear. His parents were safely in the kitchen eating dinner, leaving Henry a whole house to have fun in.

Sneak

Sneak

Sneak

Then suddenly Henry heard his parents' voices. Yikes! They were coming upstairs. Henry darted back into his bedroom and hid behind the door.

'He's in *bed*?' said Mum incredulously. 'Before nine o'clock?'

'Yup,' said Dad.

'This I have to see,' said Mum.

His parents stood outside his bedroom peeking in.

'See?' whispered Dad proudly. 'I told you, you just have to be firm.'

Mum marched over to Henry's bed and pulled back the duvet.

'Oh,' said Dad.

Horrid Henry slipped out of his room and dashed downstairs. There was only one thing to do. Hide!

'HENRY!' bellowed Dad, running down the hall. 'Where are you? Get back in bed this minute!'

Horrid Henry squeezed under the sitting room sofa. They couldn't make him go back to bed if they couldn't *find* him, could they?

'Have you found Henry yet?' he heard Dad call Mum.

'No,' said Mum.

Tee hee, thought Horrid Henry.

'Is he in the loo?' said Mum.

'No,' said Dad.

'The kitchen?'

'No,' said Dad.

'Maybe he's gone to bed,' said Mum. She sounded doubtful.

'Fat chance,' said Dad.

Henry heard Mum and Dad's footsteps coming into the sitting room. He held his breath.

'Henry . . .' said Dad. 'We know you're in here.

Come out this minute or you're in big trouble.'

Henry kept as still as he could.

Mum checked behind the sofa.

Dad checked behind the TV.

Hmmn.

'I'll check Peter's room,' said Mum.

'I'll check Henry's room again,' said Dad.

The moment they left the room, Henry leapt out and dashed to the coat cupboard in the hall. They'd never find him here.

Henry made himself comfy and cosy in the corner with the wellies. Ahh, this was the life! He'd be safe here for hours. Days. Weeks. When the coast was clear he'd sneak out for food and comics. No more school. No more bed. He'd never leave his little hidey hole until he was grown up and could stay up forever.

Uh oh. Footsteps.

Henry jumped up and dangled from the coat rail, hiding himself as best he could behind the coats.

Dad flung open the cupboard door.

Horrid Henry hung on to the coat rail. His feet dangled.

Please don't find me, thought Henry. Please, please don't find me.

Dad pawed through the coats.

Horrid Henry held his breath.

He hung on tighter and tighter . . .

Dad closed the door.

Phew, thought Henry. That was close.

CR—ACK!

CRASH!

Coats, rail and Henry collapsed to the floor.

'Hi Dad,' said Horrid Henry. 'What are you doing here?'

All was not lost, thought Horrid Henry as he lay in his boring bed with the lights off. His mean, horrible parents could make him go to bed, but they couldn't make him sleep, could they? Ha ha ha. He'd been *pretending* to be asleep. Now that the coast was clear – party!

Henry took his torch, a big stash of comic books, sweets, toys, his cassette player and a few Driller Cannibal CDs and made a secret den under his duvet.

Now, this was more like it.

'Tear down the school! Don't be a fool!' warbled the Driller Cannibals. 'Watcha waitin' for?'

'Ahh, don't be a fool!' sang Henry, stuffing his face with sweets.

'What's going on in here?' screamed Dad, flinging back the duvet.

Rats, thought Henry.

Dad confiscated his flashlight, food, comics and CDs.

'It's eleven o'clock,' said Dad through gritted teeth. 'Go to sleep.'

Horrid Henry lay quietly for thirty seconds.

'I can't sleep!' shouted Henry.

'Try!' screamed Mum.

'I can't,' said Henry.

'Think lovely thoughts,' said Dad.

Horrid Henry thought about monsters.

Horrid Henry thought about ghosts.

Horrid Henry thought about burglars.

Horrid Henry thought about injections . . .

'DAD!'

'What?'

'The hall light isn't on.'

Dad plodded up the stairs and turned it on.

'Dad!'

'WHAT?'

'My door's not open enough.'

Dad trudged up the stairs and opened it.

'Dad!'

'What?' whimpered Dad.

'Where's Mr Kill? You know I can't sleep without Mr Kill.'

Dad staggered up the stairs.

'I'll look for him,' said Dad, yawning.

'And I need to be tucked in again,' said Henry.
Dad left the room.

Horrid Henry was outraged. Humph, wasn't that
just like a parent? They nag and nag you to go to
bed and when you tell them you're ready to sleep,
suddenly they don't want to know.

Henry waited. And
waited. And waited.

The clock said 11:42.

Still no Dad. And no
Mr Kill.

'Dad?'

There was no answer.

'Dad!' hissed Henry.

Still there was no
answer.

Henry jumped out of bed. Where was Dad? He
needed to be tucked in. How could they expect him
to sleep without being tucked in?

Henry peeped into the hall.

No Dad.

Henry checked the bathroom.

No Dad.

He walked downstairs and checked the kitchen.

Still no Dad.

What a rotten father, thought Horrid Henry. To abandon his son without tucking him in . . .

Henry peeked into the sitting room.

'Dad?'

Dad was lying on the sofa holding Mr Kill and snoring.

'Hey Dad, wake up!' shrieked Horrid Henry. 'I'm ready for bed now!'

Horrid Henry's Bedtime Thoughts

No one ever wants to go to bed (unless you're a baby nappy-face wormy toad like Peter). But sometimes you've got no choice . . . so here's some great things to think about to help you fall asleep.

1. Count zombies
2. Count marauding goats
3. Think about the monster hiding under your bed
4. Think about the monsters hiding in your wardrobe
5. Listen to all the scary creaks on the stairs
6. Remember the scary vampire story you saw on TV
7. Wonder if your bathroom is haunted
8. Imagine werewolves trying to smash their way into your room
9. Remember that really spooky ghost story
10. Imagine being chased by a gigantic spider

Trust me, you'll be asleep before you know it.

HORRiD HENRY'S
Diary

Miss Battle-Axe said everyone had to keep a diary for a day. What a dumb, boring assignment! I'm not writing a single word. I've got far too much else to do. So there. You can't make me. Ha ha ha.

Oh all right. I'll write it. But never again.

8:00. am

The alarm goes off. Ignore it. No way am I going to school. I'm not going to school because I have a terrible case of Schoolatosis. Or maybe it's Schoolpox. Or Schoolplague. Ralph got Schoolitis and he got to stay home for three days!! The only cure for Schoolatosis is to stay home, eat lots of ice cream and watch loads of telly. Because let's face it, it's no fun being ill when you're too ill to enjoy yourself.

8:05

The alarm goes off again. I ignore it. I'm sick!!

8:06

Mum yells at me to get up. I hide under the duvet.

8:07

Dad yells at me to get up. I pretend it's a bad dream.

8:12

Peter comes in and says I'll be late for school if I don't get up. GOOD, I say. Naturally, he's already dressed.

8:14

Mum pulls the duvet off and screams at me to get up and get dressed NOW. I say I feel sick and I can't go to school. Mum doesn't believe me.

8:15

I heave my heavy bones out of bed. I think making children get up at the crack of dawn to go to school is a cruel and unusual punishment. When I'm king all schools will be turned into sweet shops.

8:16

I find some clothes under the bed and put them on. I can't find any socks that match so I grab some from the dirty clothes basket.

8:20

I go downstairs. Peter is already eating breakfast. He likes muesli. I like Scrummy Yummies. Mum yells at me for wearing a dirty T-shirt. Dad yells at me for not pulling my chair closer to the table. But who cares if some of my breakfast gets all over my clothes and the floor? I don't.

8.40

Yikes! I can't find my schoolbag.

8:44

I find my schoolbag. What is it doing under the sofa?

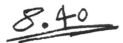

8:45

Uh oh . . . I can't find my PE kit.

8:49

I can't find my homework because I didn't do it. Oh well. Maybe Miss Battle-Axe will forget to ask us to hand it in.

I've got some great homework ideas: why watching TV is better than reading; see how much TV you can watch in a week; count how many chocolate bars you eat in a week, then subtract one every time you eat a vegetable.

8:50

We leave the house to walk to school. Dad asks me if I've brushed my teeth. Yes, I say.

8:51

I come back home to brush my teeth. We set out again.

8:53

Emergency! I've forgotten my packed lunch. We rush back to get it.

8:55

Dad, Peter and I run like mad and get to school just as the final bell is ringing at 9.05.

9:05 – 3:30

School. Work, work, work, work, work. Ugh. My best subject is lunch. I am brilliant at: eating, trading carrots for chocolate and food fights. After lunch we do more work. I get into trouble for poking William, tripping Linda, shoving Dave, pinching Andrew, copying Clare, making rude noises, chewing gum, not doing my homework and talking in class. That's not so bad. In fact, that's practically a perfect day. I bet I get mentioned in the Good as Gold Book!

3:30

School ends! Yippee!

4:00

I stretch out in the comfy black chair with a bag of crisps and switch on Rapper Zapper. Bliss.

4:12

Peter says it's his turn to watch *Daffy and her Dancing Daisies*. It's not fair!

4.22

Ralph phones. We make plans for tomorrow. I think we should raid the Secret Club biscuit tin. Ralph thinks we should stinkbomb them. I think we should do both!

4:45

I'm sent to my room for snatching the clicker and changing the channel to *Mutant Max*.

4:45 — 6:00

I read comic books.

6:01

Dad yells at me to come down and lay the table.
I don't hear him. Well, I was busy.

6:10

I come downstairs very slowly and am too late to set
the table. Boo hoo.

6:15 — 7:00

Dinner. I hate peas, so I flick them at Peter, and kick
him. When he's not looking I snatch some of his
chips. Hmmm, boy, do those chips taste great!

Mum tells me off for chewing with my mouth
open.

Dad tells me off for making a mess. Mum tells me
off for calling Peter an ugly toad and a smelly nappy.

They both tell me off for flicking peas and Peter
and for kicking him. But I'm happy because Peter
didn't notice I snatched his chips. Tee hee.

_7:10 — 8:00_

I scream and yell that I won't have a bath.

_8:00 — 8:02_

I have a bath.

_8:03_

I tell Mum I don't have any homework. This may not
be entirely true. But *if* I have homework I didn't write
down what it was, and anyway I lost the worksheet
Miss Battle-Axe *may* have handed out and there's no
point in calling Ralph because he won't know about
any homework so really I don't have any homework.

_8:04 — 8:15_

I dance around my room singing along with the
Driller Cannibals. I turn up the music as loud as I
can. Mum and Dad scream at me to make it softer.
I don't hear them – how could I? My music was
loud! They burst into my room and turn off my tape.
They are the meanest, most horrible parents
in the world and I hate them.

8:16 – 8:25

I go into Peter's room, and grab some of his toys.
Then I sneak back into my room.

8:30

Peter says I've taken some of his toys. I tell him I
haven't. Peter tells Mum. I get into trouble. BUT
I will be revenged!

8.30 — 9:00

I read a fantastic book about a great kid who is always getting into trouble and also has a horrible younger brother who's perfect and two super mean parents. I can't remember the title but I really recommend it.

9:00

Lights out. Time for my trusty torch to continue reading under the covers.

9:32

Mum confiscates my torch. Just as well I have another one!

2:23 am

Yawn. Goodnight.

ZZZZZ

PSSST!

You don't think that's my *real* complete diary, do you? Ha! Of course I couldn't let Miss Battle-Axe know every single thing I did today. I'd get into so much trouble I'd be stuck doing extra homework for 200 years and I'd be banned from the computer and the TV and . . . well, that's why I left those bits out. Heh Heh Heh. Here are the bits I cut:

Peter was being very grabby about the Comfy Black Chair this morning, so I had no choice but to push him off it. He told on me, but I got my revenge, because I have hidden the remote!!! Now only I can find it!!!! Everyone is busy right now looking for it, but will they check the shed? I don't think so!!!!! Tee hee. I think it will reappear when it's time to watch *Knight Fight*.

I didn't exactly go straight into class even though the last bell was ringing at 9.05. Instead I looked at all the election posters for school president on the playground walls. I turned Margaret into a frog and changed her election slogan to: Ribbet Ribbet. Vote Margrunt.

When I got home from school and went out to my Purple Hand Fort, I discovered we'd been raided! The biscuit tin was empty, and someone had gone through our top secret file. It could only have been the Secret Club. Well, I sneaked over there pretty quick, raided *their* biscuits, stole *their* top secret plans and left a booby trap inside. Tee hee, just wait till

Margaret and Susan go in. I put some shampoo mixed with grass by the entrance: they'll step in it and think that Fluffy threw up there.

Tonight I raided Peter's room and stole Mr Bunnykins and all Peter's sheep collection. I'm not allowed to go into Peter's room without his permission, but who cares? I heard him practising his horrible cello downstairs so I sneaked in. His room was so tidy I found it very depressing, so I have moved a few things. Well, lots of things, and now his room looks so much better. By mistake Grandma gave Peter some sweets, which Peter doesn't like, so I ate them. Hmm, boy, they were yummy. I also improved the pictures on his walls by adding a few moustaches and beards. Now his room looks really great!

HORRID HENRY'S
Top Triumphs Fact File

Making Peter believe that his time machine could travel to the future

Stealing all the chocolate from Peter's Pirate Party

Making Bossy Bill leave the School

Escaping from
Milksop Miles
and the
Happy Nappy

Beating Moody
Margaret to become
School president

Vote Henry
OR ELSE !

Winning the
Sports Day race

HORRID HENRY

By Francesca Simon

Illustrated by Tony Ross

Paperbacks with four stories each

Horrid Henry

Horrid Henry and the Secret Club

Horrid Henry Tricks the Tooth Fairy

Horrid Henry's Nits

Horrid Henry Gets Rich Quick

Horrid Henry's Haunted House

Horrid Henry and the Mummy's Curse

Horrid Henry's Revenge

Horrid Henry and the Bogey Babysitter

Horrid Henry's Stinkbomb

Horrid Henry's Underpants

Horrid Henry Meets the Queen

Horrid Henry and the Mega-Mean Time Machine

Horrid Henry and the Football Fiend

Horrid Henry's Christmas Cracker

Horrid Henry and the Abominable Snowman

Horrid Henry Robs the Bank

Horrid Henry Wakes the Dead

Horrid Henry Rocks